Operation Trenton

A Screenplay

Written by

JOHN OUELLET

ISBN 0-9748410-5-6

1

DETROIT, MICHIGAN; EXT. HART PLAZA; NIGHT

LIGHT DRIZZLE. A sniper aiming a rifle, a camouflage patrol cap low over his brow. Only his right eye and cheek can be seen.

SNIPER (WHISPERS)
There are things worth killing for.

His finger slowly squeezes the trigger.

EXT. ALLEYWAY; NIGHT; ONE MONTH EARLIER

Van door SLAMS. Black combat boots are seen stepping from a van's passenger-side door and rushing to the van's rear. Gloved hand opens the van's back doors and shines a flashlight inside. Eight men in BDUs and black Balaclava are seated. Flashlight hits each pair of eyes in turn and lingers momentarily. Door closes. Man re-enters passenger's side, nods, and the van speeds off down a dark alley.

A Grand National and a beat-up stepvan are parked near the end of that alley. Five young black men talk in the front of the cars. The van screeches to a stop behind them. Eight men scramble from van with rifles and tactically encompass the young guys.

LEAD TEAM MEMBER (SCREAMING)
Police. Down, down, down!

All go down except one, who drops a suitcase and scrambles. A team member side steps and strikes him across the back. He HOWLS and goes down on his stomach. The team member places a knee in his back and the muzzle to his neck.

BLACK MAN ON GROUND
Man, you can't be doing shit like that. You cops or feds?

No response.

BLACK MAN
Just do your thing. Don't go beatin' a...

Another team member moves in and lands the toe of his boot into speaker's face, blood SPLATTERS. Lead team member pulls him away and shoves him towards van. The two make intense eye contact. Lead team member directs others with a wave his arm. Four members move to the stepvan and form a line. Boxes are pulled from stepvan and loaded into team van as lead member grabs the discarded suitcase and places it in the front seat of the van. He unzips it and sees a stack of wrapped bills. A team member walks up beside him.

TEAM MEMBER
Two hundred grand?

LEAD TEAM MEMBER
Close enough

Team leader turns to men on ground.

TEAM LEADER
Listen up. Keep your heads down and your mouths shut until we pull you up for processing.

C.S. of black man. Van starts up. SQUEALING tires. Sound of van dissipates and man pokes his head up.

BLACK MAN
They ain't cops, mothafuckas. And they got my man's dope. I'm a dead man.

EXT. GRAVEL LOT; THE MIDDLE OF NOWHERE; DAY

EDGAR RITTENAUER, mid-thirties, 6-feet, 200-pounds; he's paunchy and dressed sloppily in blue jeans, maroon T-shirt and work boots. He's seen walking cautiously amidst a group of men and women clad in Battle Dress Uniforms (BDUs). The gathering is secluded by acres of forest and open fields. Beside a shiny, Airstream mobile trailer, he sees a well-built soldier (SERGEANT AVERY STONE) standing at attention.

INT. AIRSTREAM; BACK ROOM; DAY

COLONEL PETER ADLER, Sixth Brigade Commander, Michigan Militia, is seated behind a desk reading papers. Adler is dawning starched BDUs and looking distinguished. He's just over six feet tall, and he's trim and tanned, with his graying hair perfectly coifed. His adjutant, MAJOR CROCKER, short and waif is standing by the door.

ADLER (TO CROCKER)
Send him in.

CAPTAIN JASON BYRD, mid 20s, all-American, enters and salutes. On his right deltoid is a plainly visible tattoo of a bald eagle.

BYRD
Sir, request permission to speak before you see Sergeant Stone.

ADLER
At ease, Jason. What is it?"

BYRD
Colonel, I'd like to offer my professional opinion of Sergeant Stone.

ADLER
It's your unit, Jason, fire away.

BYRD
No, sir, it's your unit, and you have the final say,
but Stone is a loose cannon.

ADLER
Need I remind you that you handpicked him?

BYRD
I was wrong.

ADLER
I told you when you picked the team that it had to work with the ones
you selected.

BYRD
He's got the others on edge.

ADLER
And if he's out, and spills his guts?

BYRD
He's volatile, sir, not a traitor.

ADLER
Work with him, Jason. We can't afford to let him go. Bring him in.

BYRD
Yes, sir.

Byrd salutes, leaves, and returns with SERGEANT AVERY STONE,
late 20's, buzz haircut. He's cocky, the Marine poster-boy but with a
twisted machismo. He enters and salutes, sharply.

ADLER
At ease. Sergeant Stone, we have precious little time to prepare for
Operation Trenton.
We cannot afford this constant return to square one. I've received
favorable reports on you from Captain Byrd. But individual skills are
worthless outside tennis, bowling, and golf. Clear?

Stone snaps to attention.

STONE (bellowing)
Clear, sir.

ADLER
At ease and keep it down, sergeant. Finely honed teamwork is what we're about. This was a grave trespass. We were lucky the kid didn't need hospitalization. A part of me wants to know what possessed you to kick him, but...

STONE
Sir, I felt he was trying to...

Adler raises his hand.

ADLER
I don't care. You lost it and that is not acceptable. You're an outstanding soldier, no doubt about that – a credit to the movement and indispensable to the Special Ops Team. I know you'll perform up to the high standards you've set for yourself. But remember, above all else, mission has priority.

Drive on, son.

Stone salutes and gives a wry smile.

EXT. GRAVEL LOT; DAY
Edgar Rittenauer is standing alone and confused as soldiers hurry past him. His younger brother, TONY RITTENAUER, a militia sergeant, comes up to him and smiles. Tony is taller and leaner.

TONY RITTENAUER
Didn't think you'd make it.

EDGAR RITTENAUER
So this is what my brother does while everyone else is playing golf.

TONY
What ya think?

EDGAR
'Bout what?

TONY
Us. Them.

Edgar, hands in his pocket, looks around.

EDGAR
Kinda ragtag.

TONY
Ragtag, huh? We got more spunk and spit than all of sitcom America.

EDGAR (mutters)
Come to think of it... looks like a sitcom.

TONY
Give it time. I got you assigned to my unit, Bravo Company, Third Battalion.

EDGAR
Third? How many battalions you got?

TONY
Three in the Sixth Brigade.

Edgar looks around.

EDGAR
Where are they all?

A tall, lanky lieutenant walks up to them. Tony Rittenauer snaps to attention and salutes.

TONY
Sixth Brigade leads the way, sir.

LIEUTENANT
For the people. This a new recruit, sergeant?

TONY
Yes, sir, my brother, Edgar.

The lieutenant and Edgar shake hands.

LIEUTENANT
Glad you're here, Ritttanuer. We can use good men, and another Rittenauer is a real plus. Sergeant, better get him over to the Sergeant Major, then head over to the movement-to-contact site.

Edgar and Tony walk quickly across the lot to the Airstream. They talk quietly without looking at each other.

EDGAR
You been to see dad, lately?

TONY
Nope.

EDGAR
He'd really like that.

TONY (sarcastically)
Would he really, now?

At the Airstream is another man in civilian attire. CASEY KITTLE, big, soft, grandfatherly. Tony peels off to talk with a female soldier, cute, petite, with her red hair wrapped up under her BDU cap. Edgar and her catch each other's eye as he stops in front of the Sergeant Major.

INT. AIRSTREAM; COL. ADLER'S OFFICE; DAY
Rittenauer and Kittle stand somewhat at attention. Adler sits behind his
desk, hands folded on top of it.

ADLER
At ease, gentlemen. On behalf of the people of our great state, welcome
to the Michigan militia. And thank you. I don't have a canned speech to
give you. We all have our personal reasons for being here. I hope yours
are righteous and pure. Share them with the others. Solidarity with the
cause brings unity and cohesion. Now as you'll find, we are not about
guns and revolution. We've already won the rights we need to live by.
Our responsibility here is not to tear down, but to uphold... and to
rebuild... within the system. If you have designs contrary to that, we
can't use you here.

EXT. GRAVEL PARKING LOT; DAY
O.S. are SOUNDS of soldiers marching in cadence. A whistle BLOWS
in the far distance. Edgar and Casey Kittle are standing together. Kittle
is squatting down, sweating and breathing heavily.

KITTLE
Man, I could go for a beer right now.

EDGAR
You all right?

KITTLE
Yeah. Whew, is it hot or what?

EDGAR
Not really. Edgar Rittenauer.

The two shake hands while Casey is still squatting.

KITTLE
Yeah, well, that beer would be good about now.

Edgar looks around with hands on hips.

EDGAR
Now what?

KITTLE
I'm in alpha company.

Edgar watches him for a moment.

EDGAR

Mind if I ask you how old you are?

KITTLE
Sixty-four

EDGAR
Why aren't you home building a tree fort with your grandkid?

KITTLE (laughing)
Would, but they're in West Virginia

EDGAR
Why you here?

KITTLE
You heard the boss, all men got their reasons.

Kittle stands.

KITTLE
Well, best go find my unit, huh?

EDGAR
You take it easy out there.

Kittle smiles, waves back at Edgar, and walks off. Edgar follows the SOUND of the whistle down a trail, through a section of woods and into a large field where several groups of soldiers are going through tactical drills. Most are carrying hunting weapons. Edgar sees Tony standing under a tree with 6 soldiers (4 men, 2 women) sitting around him. Tony is lecturing; the soldiers are scribbling notes in small spiral notebooks.

TONY (to the group)
It's important to remain dispersed in your wedge at ten to fifteen yard intervals, depending on terrain. Only when contact is made do you move out of that formation. Why is the wedge important?

A soldier jumps up to attention.

SOLDIER (shouting)
For speed and control, sergeant.

TONY
Correct. Contact is done by bounding overwatch – which we'll cover later. Now, what . . .

PAM TROMBLEY, a female soldier in BDUs, approaches Edgar from behind. She is carrying a walking stick and a switch from a willow tree.

PAM
You a spy or are you lost, soldier?

She startles Edgar who recognizes her as the woman Tony had been talking to earlier. Tony's lecture goes on in the B.G.

EDGAR
Just watching.

Pam moves around in front of him, blocking his view of Tony.

PAM
Ah-huh. Private Rittenauer, I presume.

EDGAR
Got the name right. Not too keen on the label yet.

PAM
Well, I'm Top.

Edgar looks down at the switch and smiles.

EDGAR
That's pretty presumptuous… seeing how we just met and all.

PAM
Top. As in First Sergeant.

EDGAR
I see. I gotta salute you?

PAM
You trying to piss me off or are you really this stupid?

EDGAR
Maybe both. All this GI Joe stuff is new to me.

Pam looks back at Tony giving his class.

PAM
You serious? I would've thought he learned all he knew from his big brother.

EDGAR
None of *that* crap.

PAM
Crap, huh? I take it you didn't serve.

EDGAR
Didn't see a need to.

PAM
That's the kind of answer I'd expect from a Rittenauer.

EDGAR
What's that supposed to mean?

PAM
Don't get your sperm all twisted.

Pam turns and nods towards Tony.

He's pretty impressive.

EDGAR
He seems to know his stuff.

PAM
And he never served either. Learned on his own. Manuals, videos, lectures; separated the good from the garbage and made himself quite an expert.

EDGAR
How do you know all that?

PAM
I'm his First Sergeant; it's my job to know.

EDGAR
You gonna know all that about me, too?

PAM
You do anything worthwhile, I'll know about it.

EXT. GRAVEL PARKING LOT; DAY
Colonel Adler, glasses on, stands before the recall formation. He reads to the troops from a paper in his hands.

ADLER
What, sir, is the use of a militia? It is to prevent the establishment of a standing army, the bane of liberty. Whenever governments mean to invade the rights and liberties of the people, they always attempt to

destroy the militia, in order to raise an army upon its ruins.

Adler removes his glasses, folds the paper, and places it in his breast pocket.

Those were the words of Massachusetts Senator Eldridge Gerry – spoken during the framing of the Constitution, and it has been true for every nation, on every continent, for over a thousand years. We are not an accident; we are not outsiders; we are a necessity and we have a mandate. As you know, we'll be hosting the Division training exercise next weekend. The staff has been planning, but you, the troops, will be executing.

Adler removes his cap and walks slowly along the troop line.

The citizens of Michigan are proud of you. I am aware of the bad press we've received. Do not despair; do not abandon the cause. The threat the militia movement has warned of for decades has arrived at our door, and it is not going away any time soon. We stand ready to defend Democracy, to maintain the ideals and visions of our nation. And we have much to do. But for tomorrow, first formation at eleven hundred hours; to give all of you time to get to the church of your choice for prayer, reflection and thanks.

4

INT. WALLY'S TAVERN; NIGHT

The bar is crowded. It is a militia-regulars place. Edgar is alone at a table, sipping a beer. He is deep in thought when an open hand POUNDS the table. He looks up as Tony passes.

TONY
Order me one – no, a pitcher. Gotta take a hot piss.

Edgar stops a waitress, orders, and then continues to sip gingerly. Tony returns as the pitcher and glass arrive. He pours himself a glass.

TONY
Damn if this don't look and smell sweet after a day like today.

Edgar watches Tony down his first glass.

EDGAR
You really believe in all that nonsense, Tony?

Tony pours another and leans back.

TONY
Know what it is, Edgar? You and I are different. You're the thinker, much as us Rittenauers ever think. But I'm the doer. Gotta admit, haven't always thought about what I was doing, but…

He leans across the table.

…yeah, Edgar, I believe. I believe because, for the first time, I've been thinking about what I'm doing. And Edgar, I'm good at it.

EDGAR
Ah-huh.

TONY
Don't give me that blow-off look, bro. You're here so you must have

concerns of your own. Nine-eleven was our wake-up call, and we're not getting it. It's like listening to your murder being plotted in your own bedroom while you sit on the toilet.

EDGAR
That's not why I'm here and you know it.

TONY
Your battle is weak compared to the real problems.

EDGAR
Yeah. Well, I'll tell you one thing – I ain't about to follow around some Desi Arnaz-looking colonel?

TONY
Colonel Adler? He's a good man, bro. Owns Citadel Homes, you've seen them. Multimillionaire who doesn't need any of this. He could be on an island somewhere. Hell, he could buy an island.

EDGAR
But he bought himself a militia instead.

TONY
Bullshit! He organized the brigade five years ago, but he didn't buy a damn thing. He earned it. Matter of fact, he gives more financially than he'll ever get back. This land we use is forty acres he bought and donated. Imagine the money he could have made turning that into a subdivision. And the Airstream is his; he lets the troops use it to keep warm in the winter while he and the staff pitch a tent. He hires a lot of out-of-work soldiers, some for good, some until they get settled. He's a good man, Edgar – a very good man.

Tony refills his glass and tops off Edgar's.

The fellas seated at the bar ROAR as Pam Trombley enters the place in tight blue jeans and a white crew-neck pullover. Her auburn hair is down past her shoulders.

EDGAR
Well, will you look at Matilda the Hun.

When she arrives at the table, a lumberjack-of-a-man comes up behind her, picks her up, and swings her.

LUMBERJACK
How's the princess warrior tonight? Ready for night maneuvers?

PAM
Settle down, Too-Tall, even at my size I'm more than you can handle.

The gang with Lumberjack HOWLS and CLAPS. Lumberjack pulls out an empty chair from Edgar and Tony's table with his foot, and places Pam in it.

LUMBERJACK
She's all yours boys. Be careful, she bites. Edgar is staring at her winsomely. She ignores him as she straightens out her blouse.

TONY
Someday you'd better take him up on it or he'll bust.

PAM
You out of your mind? Imagine the diseases a thing like that carries.

She looks over at Edgar who is still staring.

PAM
Yes?

EDGAR
You do have a civil side.

PAM
I only use it when drinking in good company.

EDGAR
I see that – in a bar full of hillbillies.

PAM
Little louder, I don't think the guys in the back heard you.

TONY
Chill, Edgar

PAM
Tony, order me the usual, will you please.

She excuses herself and heads off.

TONY
What was that about? You two have a past I don't know about?

EDGAR
We met in the woods this morning. Nothing exciting – although she did show off her big stick and whip.

TONY
What?

Edgar shakes his head nevermind.

EDGAR
The usual, huh? This a regular thing for you two?

TONY
On occasion.

Tony flags down a waitress and orders a Seven and Seven.

EDGAR
Got something going on?

TONY
I wish.

EDGAR
Oh, I get it – you're making your move.

TONY
Nah.

EDGAR
If it gives you hope, she's impressed with your tactical skills.

TONY
She said that?

Edgar nods and takes a guzzle of his beer.

EXT. DOWNTOWN SACRAMENTO, CALIFORNIA; SOUTHSIDE
PARK; NIGHT

A black vehicle pulls to the curb. A young, Arab male is sitting on a
park bench. The passenger side window goes down.

DRIVER
Get in.

The Arab male sits for a second before moving. He shakes his head
slowly and sighs deeply. He stands and enters the car.

DRIVER
You set, Sammy?

SAMMY (barely audible)
Yeah.

DRIVER
What's that?

SAMMY (loudly and angrily)
I said, yes, Detective Tatum, I'm set.

DETECTIVE TATUM
Go over it again for me, Sammy.

SAMMY
You drop me off. Jamaal drives up, I say, beat it the cops are here, you pull a grenade launcher outta your pocket and blow him away.

TATUM
You little fucker. Try it right, or I'll dump you off in the middle of your raghead brethren and let them rip your ass to shreds.

SAMMY
Jamaal picks me up. I tell him I got three M-16's stashed in a culvert on Seventh & Capital. We drive there and pick up the stuff. He gives me the money, and then I meet you at the Mobil station across from the zoo. By the way, just so you know, Jamaal's only doing this because he thinks I need the money. He's into dope, but none of this shit.

TATUM
Yeah, he's a hell of a guy.

SAMMY
That's right; he is. If you didn't have me on these trumped-up charges, I'd tell you to go to hell.

TATUM
Hey, Sammy, courts are there for everyone, take your chances.

Detective Tatum drops Sammy off and drives away. He places a call on his cell phone.

TATUM
Everything's in place, lieutenant.

LIEUTENANT (V.O.)
Good. Hey, what exactly did this anonymous caller say was supposed to

go down?

TATUM
Her didn't, but if I know Sammy Al-Ghamdi, it's gonna be good.

LIEUTENANT
That's what I'm afraid of. You know, the INS building is at that intersection. We should call the JTTF.

TATUM
I don't need the feds botching up my case. Besides, it's too late now. I'll let you know how it goes down.

He disconnects and calls over his car radio.

TATUM
S-one is on the ground. Eye, is the videocamera gonna pick it up?

VOICE
Ten-four. I have the target vehicle landing. Two mutts out and moving. Looks like one has a suitcase. They're at the corner... looking down on the ground for something.

Detective Tatum pulls a black box out from under the front seat and places it on his lap. He opens it, then reaches under his dashboard and flips a switch. His siren activates.

VOICE
Who jumped the gun. They're bolting.

Tatum flips a switch on the blackbox and a deafening explosion is heard. Then all is quiet for several moments.

TATUM
Everyone all right? What happened?

VOICE
Damn, it just blew; everything is gone.

TATUM
Still have our targets in sight?

VOICE
No. Everything's gone.

5

EXT. MILITIA TRAINING AREA; DAY

Edgar is watching Tony conduct a fire and maneuver exercise in an open field with a slight upward slope. Six soldiers are walking across the field. CRACK of automatic weapons fire, and the men hit the dirt. In groups of three they double-time it at five-yard scrambles before hitting the ground again to support the second group. Two renditions and the men are exhausted, dragging their rifles, leaning on trees, just squatting instead of going onto their stomachs. Tony blows the whistle and heads out to talk to them. Pam walks up to Edgar.

PAM
Course is too long.

EDGAR
That what it is?

PAM
That, and the men are terribly out of shape.

EDGAR
They're out of their minds is what they are. You got a new guy, Casey Kittle, like seventy years old. This kind of stuff will kill him.

PAM
They fought that old in the Revolutionary.

EDGAR
No they didn't, most guys were dead by the time they hit fifty.

PAM
Anything constructive to say, Rittenauer?

EDGAR
To tell you the truth, I thought there'd be a lot more talking. You know,

discuss issues over coffee and scones, contemplate solutions.

PAM
Sounds like you wanted a poli-sci class.

Edgar shrugs.

PAM
Well, if you're staying you'll need a uniform and equipment.

EDGAR
Like what?

PAM
Most have just the basic: couple sets of BDUs, boots, web belt, suspenders, canteen, e-tool, ammo pouches. Course you could go top-of-the-line for the rucksack, jungle and desert fatigues, cold weather gear.

EDGAR
I think I'll stay with the jeans, T-shirt, and Swiss Army knife.

Colonel Adler is nearby, watching the drill.

ADLER
Sergeant?

TONY
Yes, sir.

ADLER
How long is this course?

TONY
Two hundred yards, sir.

ADLER
Make it fifty for the Division exercise.

Adler then walks off.

EDGAR (to Pam)
Hey, you're pretty good. Maybe you should play commander.

EXT. MILITIA TRAINING AREA – DUSK.
Most of the field is empty. A few remaining soldiers are filing out to their cars. Tony, looking dejected, meets up with Edgar.

EDGAR
Going over to Wally's?

TONY
No. Maybe later. I don't know.

EDGAR
Someone piss in your Corn Flakes?

TONY
You heard the colonel, telling me to shorten the course.

EDGAR
So?

TONY
So? I can't shorten it. You can't show bounding overwatch in fifty yards.

EDGAR
Course not, what are they thinking.

TONY
I need fresh troops, not a smaller battlefield. These guys out here, shit, they don't have it.

EDGAR
Big deal, it's just a game.

Tony tightens up.

TONY
A game? This ain't no game.

EDGAR
Well, you'd better hope it is – 'cause you guys would get your ass kicked.

TONY
Fuck you.

EDGAR
Got some nice sound effects, though. Sounded like real machine guns.

TONY
They were. Guys in the Guard get 'em once in a while. Blanks, though.

EDGAR
How the hell do you guys get away with so much around here?

TONY
Shit, half the brigade are cops or local officials. And we got permits and post guards. So no one screws with us. And, for what it's worth, I hope you stay on. It's good having you around. And hey, if it's the rank, tell them you're gonna quit – they'll make you a sergeant.

INT. WALLY'S TAVERN; NIGHT
Edgar comes in as Pam and two other females are coming out.

PAM
Hello there.

EDGAR (hastily)
Hi.

He quickly moves past the women and goes inside. Within a few seconds, Pam is behind him.

PAM
Tony here?

EDGAR
Geez, you're everywhere. You just kinda pop up, huh?

PAM
Something like that. Is he?

EDGAR
Huh? No. Matter of fact, I'm just coming from his house.

PAM
Eleven-thirty. Little late to be starting, isn't it?

EDGAR
Not when every night's a Friday.

PAM
That mean every morning's a Saturday.

EDGAR
Something like that. Hey, about the last time we were here, sorry if I
came off flip.

PAM
No problem, you were just flirting.

EDGAR
Was I?

PAM
Yeah.

EDGAR
Sounds about right.

EXT. RENTAL STORAGE FACILITY; DAY

Three men are walking through rows of storage lockers. The manager, an older, shorter man is leading, fumbling with a set of keys; a man dressed in a blue suit follows, accompanied by a slightly shorter, much-heavier man in a police uniform.

MANAGER
I told him I was gonna cut the lock if he didn't pay up. Tried to give him a break, he'd been here a year and always on time, but something told me he wasn't going to pay up.

MAN IN SUIT
What's his name?

MANAGER
Andy Boswell.

MAN IN SUIT   (to officer)
Know him, Chief?

CHIEF
Yeah. Local drunk. Lives down the road a piece.

The two wait behind the manager as he cuts the lock and swings the door open to reveal a pallet with duct taped packages of cocaine. The man in the suit looks over at the Chief who is staring open-mouthed.

INT. AIRSTREAM; ADLER'S OFFICE; NIGHT

Adler pounds the desk. Standing before him at attention is MAJOR GROSMEYER, Brigade Operations Officer and the Chief of Police who saw the cocaine in the storage locker.

ADLER
I don't want your thoughts on this. It was your thoughts that created this problem.

GROSMEYER
It was a good plan, sir. Boswell screwed up by not paying.

ADLER
Well, now the feds are pressing him for details.

GROSMEYER
But he doesn't know any, sir. Dumb son of a bitch thinks he's on a covert op for the DEA.

ADLER
Don't be so dismissive, Major. Fix this problem – and fix it now.

EXT. MILITIA TRAINING AREA; DAY

Division Exercise, one week later. It is extremely crowded. Groups of twenty to thirty soldiers are marching in formation. Classes are in progress: applying camouflage to face and equipment; land navigation; throwing hand grenades; laying in claymore mines; low-crawling under strands of barbed wire and hurtling over sawhorses; how to search/escort prisoners. Portable walls with windows and door frames are in place for classes on urban warfare. A live-feed reporter stands before the class on pugil sticks. The road is lined with vehicles. There are several local news vans in the parking lot.

REPORTER
Lou Carroll, reporting live. No, not Fort Bragg, North Carolina, but Hertford County, Michigan. This is the annual training exercise for the Second Division of the Michigan Militia, hosted by Hertford County's own Sixth Brigade. Never heard of them? Well, you have now.

Interviewing Adler.

ADLER
People may see our training here today as a response to the Arab terrorist bombings last week in California, but we've been here and active for five years. And I can tell you... the Sixth Brigade is ready.

REPORTER
Ready for what?

ADLER
The days of this country being an open target are done. And so are the jokes about defending ourselves. There has to come a time when you sit your child down, look him in the eyes, and tell him it's okay to defend himself. That's what we're doing; it's what the whole country should be doing. Many of our military forces, including the Reserves and the Guard, are gone – they're fighting the enemy on their own turf. Who is

home to protect America for Americans? I know it isn't popular, but it's sure as hell true – some things in this world are worth dying for.

Back to live feed.

REPORTER
Of course the bombings the colonel referred to are the two this past week which leveled the INS building in Sacramento, killing five, including the two suspected bombers, and the federal building in San Francisco that killed eleven. Just this morning we learned that a video of the Sacramento bombing may exist, and sources say it plainly shows two Arab males planting the bomb. I'm told the video was taken by County Deputies surveilling the subjects based on an anonymous tip. The area's Arab community has denied involvement or prior knowledge. But it does re-surface serious concerns about the FBI's grasp on the internal terrorist threat.

EXT. MILITIA TRAINING AREA; DAY
Edgar and Pam are in the woods off a narrow trail. She is pulling a pair of BDUs from a bag and military gear from a box. Edgar is stripping off his clothes.

EDGAR
You didn't need to do this. I told you I wasn't interested.

PAM
You can't be here without a uniform. Be like going to the prom without a tux.

EDGAR
I did that.

Edgar, his boots off, his pants down at ankles and shirt unbuttoned, picks up the BDUs.

EDGAR
They feel like cellophane

PAM
They're brand new; they'll loosen up.

He puts on the BDU hat.

EDGAR
I like the hat.

Pam looks up.

PAM
Cute.

EDGAR
This safe here? I mean, I know you all train to kill people, but I'd hate to be arrested for indecent exposure.

PAM
No one uses this part of the property. But we gotta hurry. I have to get mess out to the troops, and I'm afraid that by the time you're down to your boxers I'm gonna jump your bones.

EXT. MILITIA TRAINING AREA; SAME DAY
Adler, Major Grosmeyer, and several news cameras and reporters are walking to the training areas. It is extremely hot. Adler is moving quickly, talking in rapid fire as the crews try to keep up.

ADLER
Our training is designed to prepare citizen-soldiers to protect themselves against acts of aggression. No entity can mobilize from scratch without prior training and coordination.

REPORTER
Mister Adler...

ADLER
Son, it's Colonel Adler.

REPORTER
Yes, Colonel, I apologize. Is your unit threatening to mobilize like the California militia has?

ADLER
Threatening? Now that's a peculiar word to describe what they're doing out there... considering they're under attack. I speak for everyone in the movement when I tell you that we will not allow a one-world government like the United Nations to have its way with our country and our Constitution. Like our forefathers, we hold this truth to be self-evident, and we'll die to protect it.

REPORTER
How would you respond to those who say all that stuff is just rhetoric for the camera?

ADLER
Son, you know as much about it as I do, maybe more. If things keep going like they are, what do you see in our future?

MAJOR GROSMEYER (breathing hard)
Sir, this trail will get us there quicker.

Grosmeyer takes the lead down the trail.

EXT. MILITIA TRAINING AREA; OFF TRAIL; SAME DAY
The entourage nears where Pam and Edgar are getting ready. Pam is on her knees, tying Edgar's boots as he buttons his shirt. Pam hears them approach and looks up.

REPORTER
Colonel, you have married couples in the unit?

ADLER
We have all types from all walks.

The reporter stops and directs his cameraman to Pam and Edgar in the woods.

REPORTER
Gives them time away from the kids, anyway.

The entourage laughs, except for Adler whose jaws tighten. Edgar turns his back to them. Pam continues to tie his boot laces, occasionally glancing over at the camera.

EDGAR (whispers)
This is so humiliating.

PAM
Relax, it's not like we're naked or anything.

EDGAR
The Grand Pubaa with them?

PAM
Oh, yeah.

EDGAR
Great. That's gonna delay my promotion to general.

EXT. MILITIA TRAINING AREA; DAY
The entire Division of about 300 soldiers are sitting on a hillside that surrounds an open area. Sergeant Stone and three others are standing in the center at parade rest. All are wearing black T-shirts with the inscription "The answer is blowing in the wind" flanked by a large graphic of the American flag. Edgar has been detailed to man the lister bags. Major Grosmeyer enters the arena and takes hold of a microphone.

GROSMEYER
Been a long day. To conclude, we have Sergeant Avery Stone who'll give a hand-to-hand combat demonstration.

Stone takes the microphone and addresses the crowd. Edgar sees a litter being loaded into an ambulance. He wanders over to it and peers into the back where he sees Casey Kittle pale white with an IV in his arm.

EDGAR (to a medic)
He all right?

MEDIC
He'll make it.

Edgar leans into the back.

EDGAR
How you doing young fella?

Kittle is barely able to open his eyes.

CASEY
Hey, aren't you the guy who told me to build a tree fort for my grandkids?

EDGAR
That's me.

CASEY
Think I'm gonna go do that now.

The medic taps Edgar on the leg. Edgar smiles and winks at Casey, then backs out. The ambulance pulls away, sirens WAILING.

STONE
Give me a volunteer about my size so I can demonstrate its effectiveness.

The crowd LAUGHS and soldiers jeer each other to volunteer.

STONE
Must be one of you.

Hands on his hips, he points at Edgar.

STONE
You!

The crowd ROARS its approval. Edgar is oblivious, watching the ambulance pull away. A soldier taps his shoulder. He turns to see Stone pointing, and the crowd egging him on. He mouths that word "what" as the soldier pushes him towards Stone. As he enters the arena Stone sizes him up.

STONE
What's you name, soldier?

EDGAR
Edgar Rittenauer.

STONE (off Mike)
Rittenauer, I want you to apply firm resistance to the holds I put on you. If they become too painful, put your hand up and I'll stop. Understand?

Edgar nods.

STONE
Verbalize, soldier.

EDGAR
I got it.

STONE
Rittenauer here may not be an All-American specimen but he does have a few pounds and a couple inches on me. With the proper control techniques, I can use that to my advantage.

Stone puts Edgar into arm bar, then pulls him off balance by quickly moving his left leg back. He applies pressure to Edgar's elbow. The pain moves Edgar to his knees. The crowd APPLAUDS. Edgar instantly throws his hand up.

STONE
The tactic is to adjust your height to gain the advantage.

EDGAR (muttering)
Yeah, well – it works.

STONE
I could never have gained a foot, but I lost a foot by stepping back, pulling my adversary off balance. In this position, he is at my mercy.

Stone demonstrates strikes to Edgar's head and ribs, barely missing him with hard shots.

STONE (to Edgar)
Grab my collar with both hands.

Edgar obliges. Stone grasps Edgar by the wrists and pulls him forward. He takes Edgar's right arm and folds it behind him, forcing it upwards. Edgar's hand goes up. Stone continues his hold.

EDGAR (muttering)
My hand is up, Sergeant.

STONE
This hold gets you behind your adversary. It depends on quickness and leverage.

EDGAR
It hurts.

Stone lets go. Edgar grabs his shoulder in pain. The crowd LAUGHS.

STONE
Come up from behind and put your arm around my neck.

EDGAR
Yeah. Watch for my hand will ya.

Edgar does as directed. Stone moves back into Edgar, squats, grabs Edgar by the wrist and elbow and twists until Edgar is balancing on one leg. Edgar throws his hand up as he fights to keep from falling.

EDGAR
Damn it, sergeant, that hurts.

STONE
From this position, you can inflict maximum damage in many ways,

EDGAR
Alright. That's it, tough guy.

Stone lifts his right leg to simulate a blow to Edgar's knee. Edgar moves in and grabs Stone's testicles with his right hand, squeezing as hard as he can. He ten hoists Stone chest high and tosses him onto his back. As Stone cries out in pain from the fetal position, Edgar pins him to the ground with the sole of his boot. Crowd ROARS.

INT. WALLY'S TAVERN; NIGHT
Edgar is seated with Tony and several others. Several militia soldiers good naturedly high-five him and slap his back. The news comes on with the film from the days' events. The tavern gets quiet. They flash various scenes from the day, ending with Edgar and Stone in the hand-to-hand arena.

REPORTER
Today the Michigan Militia flexed its muscle, convinced that its services may soon be needed. Many officials are critical of their methods and politics, but with fear and suspicions mounting....

Camera zooms in on Edgar flipping Stone, ending with Edgar giving the thumbs up gesture.

REPORTER
Is it only a matter of time before the tables are turned? The bar erupts in applause. Stone is at the bar. He swivels slightly towards Edgar,

glaring.

INT. ADLER'S RESIDENCE; NIGHT
Colonel Adler is walking down a dark corridor, unbuttoning his BDU blouse. Dim lights on in a room he passes. O.S. his wife calls out in a drunken slur.

WIFE
How'd it go?

ADLER
Fine.

WIFE
The kids called. Gloria wants us to come up next weekend for a cookout.

Adler keeps walking without looking in.

ADLER
Can't. I'm tied up for the next three weeks.

WIFE
That's fine. I think I'll go.

Adler enters his rich cherry-paneled study and closes the door. He tosses his blouse onto the leather armchair. He pulls a flavored soda water from his mini-refrigerator and sits at his huge desk, facing his computer. He logs in, connects to Instant Messenger and clicks on "ColGS." His screen name comes up as "ColWol."

COLWOL
"Seeds are planted."

COLGS
"Message here is slow but on the move."

COLWOL
"Getting left wing static?"

COLGS
"Left, right, and dead center. BUT folks are listening."

COLWOL
"Don't want the details but keep us appraised of future plans."

COLGS
"Wilco. Watch for Mr. Sunshine, next in chute."

COLWOL
"Wolverine waiting in den Ex went well. Good press coverage. Anti-us, of course. All raging paranoia.

COLGS
It's just what we need."

COLWOL
"For the People. Out."

EXT. INTERSTATE 75; SAME NIGHT
Edgar is driving back from Wally's. It's nearly ten o'clock. From the left lane, he sees the exit to the militia training area. Without signally he cuts through traffic to the right, cutting off several cars.

He drives to the training area and cuts the headlights as he approaches. He parks a good distance away, and walks cautiously down a path to the gravel parking area. Headlights of a vehicle light up several men working around the Airstream. They're loading wooden crates into the back of a van. As Edgar moves closer, staying out of sight along the woodline, he overhears them talking.

SOLDIER 1
One more trip, one more trip. How many one more trips we got?

SOLDIER 2
Two, I think.

SOLDIER 1
This is bullshit. Take another hour to get them into storage.

SOLDIER 2
Better now than later.

CAPTAIN BYRD
Bitching ain't gonna get it done, soldier.

SOLDIER 1
Captain, I got to work tomorrow.

SOLDIER 2
We all do.

SOLDIER 1
Kiss ass.

CAPTAIN BYRD
Shut-up. Remember, we're doing it for Trenton.

SOLDIER 1
Wish the fuck I'd never hear of Operation Trenton.

A blue and silver Ford 150 pick-up RACES down the road from behind Edgar. He rolls into bushes as it races past. It SKIDS to a stop on the gravel. Edgar recovers to see the driver get out and run into the Airstream.

Within seconds the driver is back out, followed by a heavy-set man in BDUs who waddles out and struggles to lift himself into the passenger's side. The pick-up roars off; Edgar dips back into the bushes until it passes. As he emerges, he is poked in the back with a stick.

VOICE (harsh whisper)
Get 'em up.

Edgar jumps and turns, grabbing the stick. It's Pam.

EDGAR (heavy-breath whisper)
Jesus, you like have your own door to another dimension?

Pam looks up at him and smiles.

PAM (laughing)
Sorry. You gonna wrestle me to the ground, too?

8

INT. EDGAR'S HOUSE TRAILER; BEDROOM; MORNING

It is early. WHINE of window air conditioner unit. Edgar is awake, on his back, hands behind his head. Pam is beside him in the twin bed, her back to him. The sheet is at their waists. Pam is tight and curvaceous; Edgar's middle is wide and bloated. He looks at Pam and raises his hand to touch her. Then looks down at himself and stops, instead pulling the sheet up to his chin.

Edgar carefully leaves the bed and wraps a nearby blanket around himself, leaving the sheet on Pam. He goes to the kitchenette and turns the television on low as he makes a pot of coffee. Pam appears at the doorway momentarily, the sheet draped loosely around her.

PAM
Morning.

EDGAR (his back to her)
Didn't mean to wake you like that.

PAM
How did you mean to wake me?

Edgar, still with his back to her, hikes the blanket tighter around himself.

EDGAR
I mean the T.V. She walks around him to his front and slips her arms through the blanket.

PAM
That was wonderful; you have nothing to be ashamed of.

Edgar returns the hug halfheartedly. He stares over her head which is pressed to his chest.

PAM
What's wrong.

Edgar breathes deeply.

PAM
I see. I'm a whore.

Edgar draws back and holds her by the shoulders.

EDGAR
God no. You're a... you're a dream.

PAM
Some dream. A week ago I'm blasting at you for being out of uniform
and now I'm screwing you.

EDGAR
Don't talk like that.

PAM
You liked it last night.

EDGAR
Only when you talk about what you're doing, not what you are.

PAM
You're sweet, but love and romance don't work for me. Believe me, I've
tried.

Edgar pulls from her embrace and takes two mugs from the cabinet.

EDGAR
I don't buy that. You're wonderful. The truth is... Tony wants you.

PAM
I know.

EDGAR
You do?

PAM
He's cute, but not exactly subtle.

EDGAR
Ever been with him? Like this, I mean?

PAM
I could say yes to see if you have a jealous streak.

EDGAR
Save it, I don't.

PAM
No? He's been to my house a few times; I'll let your mind wander with the rest.

EDGAR
That's a rough area you live in.

PAM
Yeah, but I know everybody. And I pack heat.

EDGAR
Good. Rapist forgets to bring his own he can borrow yours.

PAM
I keep it in a pretty safe place. I pulled up some floor boards in my back bedroom closet.

EDGAR
And suppose he takes it out of your hands?

PAM
My hands are the safest place it can be.

EDGAR
Tony and I have been away long enough, as brothers, you know. Now that we're back, I don't know of anything worth risking that.

PAM (dejectedly)
I see.

EDGAR
I don't think you do; he's all I got left.

PAM
No other family?

Edgar pours the coffee. He gestures to the sugar bowl. Pam shakes her head, takes the cup, and drinks it black.

EDGAR
Before this summer, I hadn't seen him in about six years. We were close growing up but he had it rough with a bad marriage and lousy jobs. He took off for Texas, then to Oregon, and I don't know where else. He ever tell you about our old man?

PAM
No.

Edgar leans against the window sill while Pam sits at the small table.

EDGAR
He was a piece of work. Mom said it was his tour in Nam. I was five when he came back, eight when he left us again. Mom turned from a useless mother to a useless human being.

PAM
She alive?

EDGAR
No. Car accident – about three years ago. Tony blames dad for that, too. But I think mostly he blames himself – for not being there. It took me

ten months to track him down. Then dad showed back up.

PAM
A mess?

EDGAR
Nope. Clean and sober, with a pocketful of money and a plan.

PAM
To do what?

EDGAR
To make it right with us, he said, and I believed him. He fucked up leaving us with her, and I think he realized that. Maybe that's why I came, to finish what he started out to do. I don't know. Damn if he didn't try. He'd been in Newark working at a car detailing shop, you know, cleaning and decking out cars. Lived cheap, saved his money, and came back and bought one in Flint. Wanted his boys with him. Tony said no.

PAM
Detailing shops are big with dopers.

EDGAR
Honest people like clean cars, too. We had the shop for three years, doing great things, with legit people, until a sting operation took it away.

PAM
Was your father involved?

EDGAR
According to the courts. He's doing seventy-eight months. I've been out of work ever since. I wasn't charged, but it sure kills a résumé.

PAM
That's horrible.

EDGAR
Tony came back just before the bust. He said he was tired of traveling,

but I think he was just ready to forgive and forget.

PAM
And then he joined the movement?

EDGAR
Yeah.

PAM
You see him? Your father?

EDGAR
Yeah; Tony won't though. It's always been tough on him. He's angry at everyone. I like to think this military-thing is Tony's way of staying in touch.

PAM
He's gotten good at it, that's for sure. He's even talked about wanting to join the special operations team.

EDGAR
What's that?

PAM
Like a SWAT team. Too much testosterone if you ask me. They're never around us. Well, that's not true; Sergeant Stone, the guy you threw in the pit, he's one of them.

EDGAR
That guy's not wired right. I think I pissed him off.

PAM
Everyone pisses him off; Tony sounds like he'd fit well in there.

EDGAR
That's not what Tony needs. Or what he wants.

PAM
It may be exactly what he wants.

EDGAR
To play soldier with psychos?

PAM
I'm not a psycho.

EDGAR
No, not you. Tony's like a kid with a new toy. He's on-again, off-again.
Like his marriage and all those jobs.

PAM
So now he's committing himself, whether it's something you take
seriously or not.

EDGAR
You defending your decision or his?

PAM
We shouldn't go there – it's not going to end up pretty.

EDGAR
Probably right.

PAM
Ever been involved in a serious relationship?

EDGAR
There was this one bar I was pretty tight with for while.

PAM
Anything with legs and breasts?

EDGAR
I was engaged once.

PAM
What happened?

EDGAR
Let's see... the Marshals delivered the seizure papers on Thursday at
four o'clock; she was gone by four-fifteen. You?

PAM
I told you – it's like oil and water. I could see myself in one, though.

Silence as they sip.

PAM
So you came to the militia to be with Tony?

EDGAR
Yeah, I guess. But I don't think the place fits me. Why are you with
them?

PAM
I was recruited for my superb administrative skills.

EDGAR
Let me guess – someone told you that you have a great ass.

PAM
He wasn't that blunt. But yeah.

EDGAR
Who?

PAM
Ready for this?

Edgar shrugs.

PAM
The colonel.

EDGAR
That horny-ass. Great taste, though. I don't think it's a good fit for you, either.

PAM
You are the jealous type.

EDGAR
No. Just don't think it's a good fit. Something's not right about them.

The news is on the television. The newscaster mentions Pine Bluffs. Both turn to watch. A reporter is interviewing Police Chief Grosmeyer. They are standing on the side of the road; a blue and silver Ford 150 pick-up is in the background.

PAM
Hey, that's Major Grosmeyer, our S-3.

EDGAR
Really? He Chief of Police here.

PAM
Chief? I knew he was cop, but the chief...

EDGAR
Not much in a town like this.

CHIEF GROSMEYER (to reporter)
Of course the investigation isn't complete. But it looks as if the victim was walking too close to the roadway. Being designated a natural beauty road by the state, this is a very dark and narrow stretch with a lot of vegetation. We've never had a fatality here before, but I can attest to lots of wildlife being hit.

REPORTER
Has the victim been identified?

CHIEF
Yes, and his family's been notified. He's a longtime resident of this

area.

REPORTER
Can you release the name to us, Chief?

CHIEF
I don't see why not. Andrew Boswell, fifty-eight years old.

REPORTER
Thank you, Chief.

Reporter turns back to the camera as Chief Grosmeyer leaves the screen.

REPORTER
The fatal accident occurred at around eleven-thirty last night. We were told earlier that the off-duty police officer who struck Mister Boswell was driving this Ford Pick-up seen behind me. He was returning from a friend's house. Reports we received say his blood-alcohol level was well within the permissible range.

EDGAR
That's bullshit, I saw...

Edgar looks at Pam who is waiting for him to finish.

PAM
You what?

EDGAR
Nothing. I thought I knew the guy, that's all.

PAM
You saw him this weekend at drill. He was with the colonel when we were in the woods.

She stands and steps into Edgar's arms.

PAM
I should get going. Trucking companies tend to seize up without their

dispatchers.

EDGAR
What's Operation Trenton?

PAM
Beats me. Where'd you hear it?

EDGAR
Last night. The men at the trailer were talking about it.

PAM
Never heard of it.

Pam slowly withdraws from Edgar's embrace and saunters into the bathroom. There is a knock on the front door. Edgar answers. It's Tony who bursts in, excited.

TONY
Guess who just got a job at Citadel?

EDGAR
Thought you already had one there?

TONY
You, you moron. I got you one with heavy equipment; your real work before that fiasco with dad.

Tony spots Pam's BDU cap with the first sergeant insignia on the kitchen table. His eyes lower and he bobs his head slowly.

TONY
So, ah, get on down to see them when you get a chance, huh.

EDGAR
Tony…

TONY
Today would be best. Coupla other guys put in but I got you a hook.

Tony shuffles out the door. Edgar follows him to the stoop.

EDGAR
Tony.

Tony keeps walking to his truck. Edgar comes back inside. Pam is standing at the bathroom door, still wrapped in the sheet.

PAM
Oops.

Edgar places his hands on the kitchen table and leans over, looking down at her cap.

PAM
I'm sorry.

He turns to face her.

EDGAR
You didn't do anything wrong. That's the problem.

9

EXT. EXXON GAS STATION; HIGHWAY 1; FORT PIERCE, FLORIDA; DAY

HALA SADAT, a twenty-five-year-old Syrian man with a thin build and a baby face, is reading a phone number from a slip of paper and dialing it into a payphone. He has a heavy middle-eastern accent.

HALA
Me.

VOICE
Got the key?

HALA
Yes.

VOICE
Locker eighty-three at the Greyhound terminal in Jacksonville.

Hala is scribbling on the scrap of paper.

VOICE
Drop off that package at nine tonight at the Shell station at Timuquana and Davison.

HALA
Yes.

VOICE
And don't tamper with it. It's sealed and if the seal's broken, you're contact won't take it. Got it?

HALA
When do I get the money?

VOICE
When you do everything you're told.

EXT. NORTH ON HIGHWAY A1A; DAY
Hala drives his old Chevy Impala at the speed limit. The windows are down, sunglasses on, Jimi Hendrix's *Hey Joe* blaring. He reaches the Greyhound Bus terminal in Jacksonville, cruises the parking lot several times, and then parks. He casually goes to locker 83 and takes out a soft-sided suitcase. It is obviously heavy but he tries to make it look light as he carries it to the car. He heaves it into the trunk and departs. He drives onto Highway 17, passing signs to the Jacksonville Naval Air Station. He drives through the Shell Station, and, seeing no one, pulls out. He's turning around in a parking lot when he sees a red pick-up truck with 2 soldiers in it, talking on a portable radio. Traveling back up the boulevard, he sees in his rearview mirror that they are following. As he nears an intersection, he sees another pick-up with 2 more soldiers merge in behind him. As it merges, he notices a placard on the door, "Florida Militia Patrol." He presses the gas pedal to the floor and cuts through a strip mall parking lot. He cuts behind the mall and heads down the narrow back alley. There is a parked van and a dumpster, making a space barely wide enough for his Impala. He attempts to squeeze through but is wedged between them. He checks his rearview mirror. No one has followed him in. He squeezes out the driver's side window and sees the red pick-up bearing down from the front. He draws a handgun from his waistband. He stops when he hears a voice on a loud speaker from behind.

VOICE
Freeze. Police. Put the weapon down. Slowly.

Without turning, he does as directed as the pick-up comes to a stop in front of the Impala. Another police car arrives and they take control of Hala, spreading him onto the hood of the squad car. They take his wallet and an officer leafs through it.

OFFICER
This you? Hala Sadat?

HALA
Yes.

OFFICER
Your car?

HALA
No, just delivering it for a man.

OFFICER
Got a name?

HALA
Pasqual Ramirez. Go ahead, check, it's on the rental agreement.

OFFICER
No doubt. What's inside.

HALA
Nothing.

OFFICER
Must be something; big enough you gotta carry a piece. Mind if I take a look?

Hala, still leaning on the hood of the squad car, shrugs. The officer goes into the car and takes the keys out of the ignition. He fumbles through them, pops the trunk, and slides the suitcase towards him. A militia soldier approaches.

SOLDIER
Officer?

OFFICER
Yeah.

SOLDIER
I wouldn't get too close to the suitcase. We've received intell that it may

contain explosives.

OFFICER
Yeah, well, I got better intell says he's got about five keys of coke. Now you right-wing Boy Scouts have done your civic duty for the day; why not take ten and let us do ours. The officer breaks the suitcase's plastic seal and unzips it. Quickly, as if he's uncovered a cobra, he jumps back.

OFFICER
Sweet Jesus, everyone get the hell out of here. Call the precinct to cordon of the block.

SECOND OFFICER
What the hell you got back there?

The first officer looks over at the militia soldier.

OFFICER
And I guess we'd better alert the naval air station; looks like we got ourselves a bomb.

10

INT. MCNAMARA FEDERAL BUILDING; DETROIT; EVENING

It is nearing six o'clock. Special Agent WINSTON AMBROSE, FBI, Detroit Field Office is meticulously, but quickly, stacking folders onto the corner of his desk. He is dressed in a white shirt with tie, sleeves rolled to his forearms. He is an intense man, late thirties, attractive, athletic build. His phone rings. Winston picks up, cradling it with his chin as he continues to stack and sort.

WINSTON
Ambrose.

The voice on the other end cannot be heard by audience.

WINSTON
Can't you take it? I'm on my way out. I know I have emergency response, this such an emergency? Yeah, they all think so. Fine, but if he wants to tell us where Jimmy Hoffa's buried, you're coming in to take copious notes.

Winston goes to the waiting room where Edgar Rittenauer is seated.

WINSTON
Can I help you?

INT. PAM'S DISPATCH OFFICE; SAME EVENING

Pam is on phone. Listening to Edgar's away message. "I'm not here. Speak."

PAM
Been over a week since you said I wasn't a whore. Gonna sweet talk a girl like that you should at least return her calls. Well... I'd really, really

enjoy getting together again, and ah, call me. Okay?

She hangs up and drums her desk with her fingertips.

INT. MCNAMARA FEDERAL BUILDING; DETROI; SAME EVENING

Winston and Edgar are in a small interview room. Bare walls, gray metal desk between them.

WINSTON
Go by Ed?

EDGAR
No.

WINSTON
Okay... What's this urgent info?

EDGAR
Well, first off, I'm not a big fan of you guys, and I'm not real comfortable being here.

WINSTON
Most folks aren't. Being here in cuffs and getting printed makes them even less friendly. But you, well, it's your quarter, you can talk or walk.

EDGAR
Yeah. Just wanted you to know, that's all. Remember a fatal car accident about a week ago... up in Pine Bluffs?

WINSTON
No, car crashes don't get on our radar screen. Less we're in them.

EDGAR
Yeah. Well, the locals investigated, and I don't think they investigated very well.

WINSTON
Why's that?

EDGAR
The Chief of Police said the guy involved was one of his officers... said the guy was with friends all night. But I saw that guy and the Chief just an hour before the crash. And they were in that same pick-up... the one that killed this guy.

WINSTON
Hmm. Sure it was the same guys, same truck?

EDGAR
I wouldn't drag my tired ass down here if I wasn't sure.

Winston looks around and takes a scrap of paper from the trash and a pen from his pocket, and poises to write.

WINSTON
Names?

EDGAR
Grosmeyer – that's the Chief. There are other witnesses, too, but don't go asking them anything, they hate you guys worse than I do.

WINSTON
Some sort of hate fest?

EDGAR
Yeah, you might say that.

WINSTON
Would I know of it?

EDGAR
I'm not here to talk about that.

WINSTON
Fair enough. Will you testify is court?

EDGAR
No.

WINSTON
I'll probably get back to you. Any particular code name you want?

EDGAR
I live alone, and I'm out of work, which you guys should already know.
So just leave your name.

WINSTON
Phone and address?

EDGAR
248-562-3215. Sixteen-0-five Bluegill Circle, lot seven, Pine Bluffs.

WINSTON
I don't know if we'll be able to do much. No one to testify and all. But
this works out, we can flip you a few bucks.

EDGAR
I'm out of a job, and I don't dress well, but what makes you think I'd
take your money.

WINSTON
I guess I know now you wouldn't.

EDGAR
Then you and I are straight, Ambrose.

11

INT. AIRSTREAM; ADLER'S OFFICE; NIGHT

Colonel Adler is meeting with Major Grosmeyer and Captain Byrd. All are in civilian clothes.

BYRD
I could use at least two more pairs of night vision goggles.

GROSMEYER
Can't. Budget got shot to hell when DEA took the dope. How about your National Guard contact?

ADLER
No. Save him for weapons and ammo. No sense burning him for something we can buy at Walmart.

BYRD
Guess we'll need another dope raid.

ADLER
Got one in the works?

BYRD
No, sir, but this is Detroit. Shouldn't take much digging.

EXT. AIRSTREAM; NIGHT

A dark figure is walking slowly along the side of the Airstream.

VOICE
Freeze. State your business.

A flashlight shines on the face of Pam Trombley. She squints into it. She's in civilian clothes, as well, hair down and full, looking nothing like a soldier. A guard in civilian clothes comes up to her, flashlight still in her face.

GUARD
What are you doing here? This is a private area.

PAM
I'm a First Sergeant in this unit.

The man leans in to get a better look at her.

GUARD
No drill tonight.

PAM
I want to speak to the colonel.

GUARD
What about?

PAM
You really think you have a need to know, soldier?

GUARD
Wait over there, by the tree line.

INT. AIRSTREAM; ADLER'S OFFICE; SAME NIGHT

A knock on the door. Adler holds his hand up to halt the conversation.

ADLER
Enter.

GUARD
Sir, sorry to disturb you but there's a woman outside who wants to speak to you.

Adler stands, walks over to the small window and peers out. He sees Pam walking by the woodline.

Say she's a first sergeant. I can send her off.

ADLER
No. I'll handle this.

Adler excuses himself and walks out to her.

I missed you after the Division exercise.

PAM
Peter, I can't stay long. I tried calling you at home.

ADLER
I wish you wouldn't do that.

PAM
There's something I need to tell you.

ADLER
Oh? Someone else? Something to do with that incident in the woods?

PAM
Peter, of course it's someone else. It's me, it's your wife, it's you in that uniform, it's every guy I meet and don't meet.

Adler looks toward the Airstream, then moves her closer to the trees and presses up against her. He talks softly and smoothly.

ADLER
Let's spend some real time together. My wife is gone for a few days.

Pam nudges away.

PAM
I need to move on, Peter.

ADLER
What if I were to tell you I was leaving her?

PAM
You don't give up, do you?

ADLER
Tonight. Just let's see how it works.

The guard is about ten yards away and peers into the darkness at them.
Pam sees him and quickly turns to Adler.

PAM
So how's Operation Trenton going?

Adler seizes her roughly by the shoulders.

PAM
Peter, you're hurting me.

GUARD
Everything okay back there, sir?

ADLER
Fine, son, go back to the trailer.

The guard walks off.

ADLER
Where'd you hear that?

PAM
Let me go.

Adler releases.

PAM
Damn, Peter, I was just trying to change the subject because the goon

came up.

ADLER
Sorry. It's just an upcoming division thing. It's not supposed to be out to the troops yet. Guess we had a security lapse. Wait for me until I'm done here. Please.

INT. ADLER'S BEDROOM; NIGHT

Adler is asleep. Pam is lying on her side, facing away from him. His arm is draped across her hip. She glances up at the clock. It's 2:45 AM.

She rolls her head back to look at him. Figuring him to be fast asleep, she slips from under his arm and moves out of the room. She is dressed in a long, white T-shirt. She goes downstairs to his study. The computer is on but the monitor screen is off. As she moves some papers, she bumps the mouse and the screen comes to life. She panics momentarily and shuts the study door. She goes through several drawers and finds a binder labeled, "OpTrent."

Taking the binder out, she reads.

PAM (muttering)
Situation... Mission... Holy shit.

She closes the binder and hastily searches the room for an object to put over the monitor. She sees Adler's BDU blouse and drapes it over the screen. Carefully, she opens the study door and takes the OpTrent binder to the back-door entrance where she places it in a trash container.

She scurries back to the stairs, starts to climb, remembers the blouse over the monitor, and returns to the study to remove it. She puts the blouse where she found it and gives the room a quick once-over.

As she exists the study and takes her second step toward the staircase, Adler yawns noticeably as he enters the kitchen. Over his shoulder, Adler looks deliberately at Pam.

ADLER
Couldn't sleep?

PAM
Thirsty. Stole a glass of OJ.

Adler smiles disingenuously, looking into the open trash bin and seeing the carton of OJ he'd finished night before.

INT. MCNAMARA FEDERAL BUILDING; FBI OFFICE; MORNING

Winston Ambrose is pouring coffee as his supervisor, CRAIG OSBORNE, enters. Osborne is late 40s, graying hair, slightly overweight. He's carrying his suitcoat over his shoulder, head down, feet shuffling along the carpet. Only a few agents and clerks are in.

OSBORNE
Terrorists suck.

WINSTON
Anyone in particular.

OSBORNE
All of 'em.

WINSTON
That's not very sensitive of you – stereotyping a whole group like that.

Osborne nudges in between Winston and the coffee. He pours and fixes.

OSBORNE
Why you here so early?

WINSTON
Not. It's eight-thirty.

OSBORNE
Huh? Yeah – damn line out there. I was in it for over an hour. Federal buildings and military posts being blown up... security lines to get into every damn thing from the post office to the crapper at the Seven Eleven. Like I said, terrorists suck.

Winston takes his coffee over to his desk. Osborne follows and picks up a report from Winston's desk.

OSBORNE
What's that?

WINSTON
Started out as a fatal traffic accident.

OSBORNE
We don't work traffic, Winston.

WINSTON
I know that. But there's a possible public corruption angle to it.

OSBORNE
Shit, man, I'm sweltering in line with four hundred pound IRS clerks because terrorists are pounding at us. Don't saddle me with Michigan politics. Farm it out to the state police.

Winston stares disbelievingly at Osborne.

WINSTON
You're kidding.

OSBORNE
Priorities are terrorism, terrorism, and more terrorism.

WINSTON
There is other crime out there, you know.

OSBORNE
You'd think so, wouldn't you. Tell you what, HQ's coming in with some top secret case. SAC wants me to head it up, and I just found my case agent.

WINSTON
Serious.

OSBORNE
Sure. Give you something big to tell the wife and kids. Winston's phone

rings. He answers.

WINSTON
Ambrose.

VOICE
Healy, DEA. You called about my agent impersonation complaint.

WINSTON
Yeah, thanks. Might be a moot point now.

HEALY
I'll say.

WINSTON
I was looking it over and noticed a Chief Grosmeyer was involved. What's he about?

HEALY
Seemed helpful. Why? He looking to join you guys.

WINSTON
No.

HEALY
Good. He doesn't do much for the image.

WINSTON
I got some info he may be dirty.

HEALY
Can't help you there, just met him the once. But now that my only witness is gone, don't think I'll be dealing with him much.

WINSTON
Gone?

HEALY
Yeah. Thought that's what you meant by "moot point." Andy Boswell.
Poor slob was run down; by an off-duty cop, no less.

WINSTON
You shitting me?

HEALY
Nope. The guy was an old rummy storing coke for a guy he thought was
with the DEA. But other than the phony name, all he gave us was the
guy's description if you're still interested: white male, tattoo of an
American Eagle on his right arm, looks like a Chippendale dancer.

Winston jots down notes.

WINSTON
Hey, thanks for calling.

Winston hangs up.

OSBORNE
So, his witness dead or go to the dark side?

WINSTON
Dead.

OSBORNE
Tank the corruption case?

Winston looks up at him.

WINSTON
That is the corruption case.

INT. ADLER'S HOME; KITCHEN; MORNING

Adler sits at his desk in the study, and taps the keyboard's spacebar – the monitor glows. He points and clicks as he reads, absently sipping from a glass of tomato juice. He places the glass on a coaster and reaches down to pull out a drawer.

He reaches in blindly while still reading. When he realizes the binder is not there, he stops reading and rifles through the various drawers' contents in earnest, one after the other. He slams the last drawer closed.

ADLER
That bitch.

INT. PAM'S DISPATCH OFFICE; DAY

Pam is tapping and chewing on a pen while sitting at her desk. She's nervously looking at the phone. She dials a phone number. No one answers. She grabs her purse and a small cardboard box. She opens the door to an office behind her.

PAM
Need a few hours. I'll be back by three. If I get any calls, tell them... No, wait. Tell them I'm busy, that I'll call back. But get a name and number.

JOE (O.S.)
What, I'm your secretary now?

PAM
Just do me this favor, okay?

She runs to her car and places the cardboard box in her trunk, then drives out of the parking lot.

INT. MCNAMARA FEDERAL BUILDING; FBI OFFICE, DETROIT; SPECIAL AGENT IN CHARGE (SAC) CONFERENCE ROOM; AFTERNOON

The conference room is austere: a long, wooden table set with 12 chairs. The U.S. and Michigan flags are at one end. On the back wall is the FBI emblem. On the far wall are photos of the past Detroit SAC's.

Winston is seated by himself at the far end of the table. Craig Osborne is seated up front with SAC HAL WARDEN. Supervisor TOM CORRAL, FBIHQ, Head of the Domestic Terrorism Unit, is standing in front of the table. Several other supervisors are seated. An agent is handing out tabbed packets to each attendee.

Winston picks his up, and notices tabs labeled, CALFBOMB, MILITIA, FLABOMB, CI INTELL. He sees he is the only person handling it so casually, and lets it drop to the desk.

CORRAL
"Guardrail," as we're calling it, is to be handled as Top Secret. Each packet is numbered. I'm passing around a roster for your name and assigned packet number. Not that we don't trust you, but… oh hell, we don't trust you.

Group laughs lightly. Roster is passed as Corral continues.

CORRAL
The packets are tabbed; the details are self-explanatory – so I won't talk you to death. Basically, there have been two bombings in California and one suspected attempt in Florida. Sixteen people are dead, twelve are injured.

WARDEN
Suspected? I thought we caught the guy in Florida red-handed?

CORRAL
Yeah. I'll get to that. Originally, it was believed that the Sacramento device was inside the briefcase, based upon the videotape everyone has seen more times than your kids have seen <u>Toy Story</u>. But at the scene, the case was largely recovered and pieced together. That wouldn't have been possible if the bomb was inside.

WARDEN
So this whole thing was a set up?

CORRAL
Lets just say... it appears that insufficient evidence has led to an inexact conclusion.

WARDEN (smiling)
Does Sacramento County know that?

CORRAL
None. Here's the rest of it in a nutshell. Look at tab C. The two principals involved were Jamaal Zibri and Samir Al-Ghamdi. Zibri had an uncle involved in the PFLP General Counsel – a violent Palestinian Liberation group. We originally thought Jamaal was a planted terrorist, but soon realized he's just a good old-fashioned coke dealer. Al-Ghamdi was his main runner, and a snitch. Deputy Harvey Tatum operated Al-Ghamdi. According to Sacramento, an anonymous caller told Tatum that Al-Ghamdi was up to something but never said what, only where and when.

WARDEN
Convenient.

CORRAL
Even more convenient? He was running it with Zibri.

OSBORNE
His dope buddy.

CORRAL
Exactly. So where was the dope? We've got credible information that

Zibri was happy enough as a trafficker; and we know he was making serious money running coke. So why become a martyr? Tab D is the kicker. The militia movement.

OSBORNE
Didn't they dry up when the Berlin Wall went down?

CORRAL
Hardly. They've been making noises since Waco and Ruby Ridge. We suspect they're getting louder now.

WARDEN
They're behind the bombings?

CORRAL
Not sure.

WARDEN
Getting close?

CORRAL
Yeah, I think. Deputy Tatum is active in the California Militia. We don't think that's a coincidence. Nor do we think it was their highly-refined surveillance tactics that led the Florida Militia to that bomber. Like Zibri, the kid was a major drug mule down there. Why blow a good gig for some radical fundamentalists? He says he was set up and we believe him.

WARDEN
Florida authorities in on it?

CORRAL
Not yet.

WARDEN
Why's that?

CORRAL
Ahh, tab E, CI Intell. Boston Division developed a confidential

informant in Nashua, New Hampshire. This guy was in the Tenth Mountain Division with a hotshot soldier – one Jason Byrd. Byrd's military photo, bio, and physical description are in the packet. His military record is impeccable. Problem was his widowed mother fell very ill and she requested his return, being the only child. He was on his way to Special Forces and had to be ordered out. He came home to Michigan, joined a local PD and the Hertford County militia. In e-mails to the CI – this Byrd talks about his local militia unit's access to weapons from nearby armories.

WARDEN
Any reported armory thefts in the recent past?

SUPERVISOR
No, sir.

CORRAL
Byrd also brags that something big is imminent. What that "something" is, we don't know.

WARDEN
Tatum and Byrd somehow connected?

CORRAL
Not directly, and they're not even our focal point. Flip through tab E to Peter Adler.

The group flips the pages. Winston is still on Byrd. He notes the section on Scars, Marks, Tattoos: "American Eagle on right deltoid."

CORRAL
Now it could be I've wasted a lot of time and resources on this; God knows it wouldn't be the first time. But this guy's the reason I'm here talking to you. He's the commander of the Hertford County militia. Back ten, twenty years ago we picked his name up at various protest rallies against flying the UN flag on state capital buildings, accepting Cuban refugees, indicting Oliver North, Supreme Court decision on flag burning. He dropped off the radar screen until just recently. He owns

Citadel Homes here in Michigan.

WARDEN
I've heard of it.

OSBORNE
I live in one.

CORRAL
Good-sized operation. He's wasn't pegged as a money man in the past,
but he's got enough of it. That, and he runs Citadel Homes as a model of
right-wing values. Mandatory drug testing, all non-union.

WARDEN (sarcastically)
Must make him real popular in Michigan.

CORRAL
Don't think he much cares. He even published a monthly political
newsletter put together by a former staffer from The American Spectator.
I read a few issues – inciting stuff. All that's missing is the swatstika.
More specific to this case, he's made several trips to San Jose and
Tallahassee in the past year. He's commanding the same militia outfit
Byrd claims is tapping armories.

WARDEN
I'm embarrassed, Tom. He's in my backyard and you know more about
him than I do.

CORRAL
You never had a reason to know him, before now. The movement's
gaining strength and support. Major cities are asking for their help and
services. Point a finger at them now and they get a bigger soapbox.
Peter Adler is a dynamic guy, a real leader. I think he's the key. He's
intelligent and connected. Essentially, it's a large domestic terrorism
operation. Some say war is the final option. But we know terrorism is.
For unlike war, it is total breakdown. Everyone is a combatant,
everything is a target.

WARDEN
How is it all connected?

CORRAL
That's what we need to know. We need to get inside. Any questions?

AMBROSE
Yeah, I got one. Does anyone else think the guy looks like a Chippendale dancer?

16

INT. FAMILY RESTAURANT; DAY

Adler is sitting alone at a table. He is watching through the front window as a black Ford Explorer parks in the lot outside. The truck's window stickers read "Rush for President" and "Don't see no black, brown, or yellow in this red, white, and blue." Avery Stone exits. He's wearing tight blue jeans and a tight short-sleeved shirt. He enters and sits down with Adler.

ADLER
Must you always walk in like a character from Deliverance?

Stone shrugs, calls out to the waitress.

STONE
Coffee.

ADLER
You don't have time; there's been a breach.

INT. PAM'S CAR; DAY

Pam is waiting in the trailer park, outside Edgar's trailer. She looks at her watch and dials him up on her cell phone.

PAM
It's around noon, Edgar. I've been sitting in front of your trailer for an hour. You won't call back and you're not home. I don't know if you even live here anymore. If you do, call. That Operation Trenton you were talking about, I was with... no, forget about how right now, but I got it, and Edgar, if it's not just talk, this is big. I can't keep it much longer and I'm scared. They know I have it – I'm sure of that. I'm putting it in that safe place until I can get it to you, so please, please call.

INT. DETROIT FBI OFFICE; DAY

Edgar is in an interview room. He's alone, sitting nervously. Winston comes in with a cup of coffee and hands it to Edgar. Osborne follows him in. They sit behind the gray metal desk opposite Edgar.

WINSTON
'Preciate you coming in on short notice.

EDGAR
No problem.

Winston glances over at Osborne.

WINSTON
You told me last time that you are a member of an organization.

Edgar looks at the two.

EDGAR
And?

OSBORNE
Which one?

EDGAR (to Winston)
Who's he?

WINSTON
Craig Osborne, my boss.

EDGAR
Well I remember last time telling you I wouldn't talk about that. Besides, I'm no longer with them.

OSBORNE
Then you can tell us who they are.

Edgar takes a slow sip of coffee.

We've done some checking. You've had some legal troubles in the past and were never formally charged.

EDGAR
That's right.

OSBORNE
Statute of limitations hasn't run on you yet.

Edgar stands. Winston stands with him.

WINSTON
Sit down, Edgar. Please.

Edgar sits. Winston looks tight-lipped at Osborne.

WINSTON
We're not investigating any groups. We're only asking questions about that accident up north... and about a few other matters.

EDGAR
Like what other matters?

WINSTON
I can't tell you that. Is Chief Grosmeyer part of the organization we're talking about?

Edgar lowers his head and remains silent.

WINSTON
Don't defend what doesn't need defending, Edgar.

EDGAR
I happen to believe there are a great many things in this country that need defending.

WINSTON
So do I. That's why I'm here. It's why we're all here. So let me start off. I think you're a member of the militia movement.

EDGAR
If I was?

WINSTON
I'd like to ask you some questions.

EDGAR
And you say that's not an investigation?

OSBORNE
It's not.

EDGAR (to Osborne)
And when the Lions play the Bears that's not a football game. Listen, you guys seem pretty decent...

Edgar glances over at Osborne.

EDGAR
...but I don't trust you.

OSBORNE
Sounds like militia talk to me.

EDGAR (to Osborne)
There are plenty of people out there that don't trust you – not just militia freaks.

EXT. WINSTON'S BUREAU CAR (BUCAR); INTERSTATE 94; EVENING

Winston is driving; Osborne is on the passenger's side.

WINSTON
Little rusty on the interviewing techniques, Craig.

OSBORNE
Guy's an asshole.

WINSTON
An asshole who could have been a good snitch.

OSBORNE
An asshole is never a good snitch.

WINSTON
Maybe in your day. Now, assholes make the best snitches.

They pull into a restaurant parking lot.

INT. RESTAURANT LOBBY; EVENING

They are both dressed in suit and tie. Winston checks out the lobby while Osborne checks out the lounge.

OSBORNE
It's mobbed.

WINSTON
Yeah. And on a weekday. I got two little kids… best we can manage is the Mickey Ds across the street.

OSBORNE
What's this guy Chambers look like again?

WINSTON
White male, six-two, two-forty-five. See him?

OSBORNE
Yeah, about ten of him.

They take a two-person table in the back. They scan the crowd as a waitress comes by. Osborne waves her off.

WINSTON
I could have used an Iced-tea.

OSBORNE
These full-time undercover agents – damn cowboys, all of them. Know how other feds hate us because they couldn't get into the Bureau? I bet UC's hate actors for the same reason.

WINSTON
They said he's the best.

OSBORNE
Watch him – that's all I'm saying. The bar area is full. Background pop music. A lot of noise, talking, laughing. A big man with long hair in a pony tail and a bushy black beard is leaning on the bar, flirting with the cute, young bar maid at the waitress station.

OSBORNE
Look at that buffoon. Some people have no self respect.

WINSTON
I had a college buddy who did that stuff, said it worked at least 10% of the time. "Shotgun approach" is what he called it.

OSBORNE
Exactly, so why do it?

WINSTON
For that one-in-ten, I guess.

They watch the man laugh, drink, and whisper to most of the women that pass by. Some seem annoyed; some just ignore him. He is undaunted.

OSBORNE
What time you got?

Winston checks his watch.

WINSTON
Six-twenty. Maybe he's in the dining room eating.

OSBORNE
They told us the lounge, right? Uh, I'll go check. That loud-mouth dick is getting on my nerves, anyway.

Osborne leaves. Winston watches the show at the waitress station. The man looks at his watch, looks over his shoulder, then catches Winston's eye, and winks. Osborne returns and sits.

OSBORNE
Nope.

WINSTON
That guy at the bar look gay to you?

OSBORNE
I can't tell anymore.

WINSTON
Well if he isn't, then I think that loud-mouth dick is our UC.

INT. PAM'S HOUSE; EVENING

Pam is sitting at her small laminated kitchen table, sipping a bottle of beer. Smooth jazz plays softly on the radio. She stares off into a corner, absently peeling the label from the bottle. A telephone sits on the corner of the table. She picks it up and makes a call.

PAM
Edgar, last shot at this before I go somewhere else. Please meet me at Wally's tonight.

She hangs up as she hears a sound in her living room. She listens for a moment, then slowly rises. She moves towards the sound.

The living room is small and she can see it all from where she stands. Convinced and relieved no one is in there, she relaxes.

She partially turns and a huge arm wraps around the top of her head and twists it. A machete slices deep across her neck. She makes a gurgling sound, her body slumps to the floor.

Stone stands above her. He stares raptly down at her dead body. He strokes the machete blade, his fingers caressing the blood. He turns to the phone and smiles.

INT. RESTAURANT; DINING TABLE; EVENING

Winston and Osborne are watching as their undercover agent, DEXTER CHAMBERS, pours the rest of the beer out of a pitcher. He holds the pitcher aloft.

CHAMBERS
You guys still on duty?

OSBORNE
Yeah.

CHAMBERS
Oh. Am I?

Osborne waves for him to continue. Chambers takes a swallow. A tall, young woman walks past.

CHAMBERS
That's a tall one, but I bet she's worth the climb.

Winston smiles. Osborne clears his throat.

OSBORNE
I don't have all night.

Chambers redirects his attention to Osborne.

CHAMBERS
Course not. You're a very busy man.

OSBORNE
You have a grasp on the project?

CHAMBERS
It's a militia thing, right?

OSBORNE (sarcastically)
Yeah. And I see you're dressed for the part.

Chambers leans back, tugs on his beard and grins broadly.

What were you doing before this?

CHAMBERS
Sorry chief, that's on a need-to-know basis. Now, how 'bout you fellas tellin' me what I need to know.

OSBORNE
This is sensitive. Don't you have a hotel room.

CHAMBERS
Sure do.

The three get up to leave. Chambers taps Winston as they pass the waitress station.

CHAMBERS (to Winston)
Wait a sec.

He returns to a waitress and whispers in her ear. She whispers back and Chambers comes over to Winston.

CHAMBERS
Okay, let's go.

WINSTON
What she say?

CHAMBERS
She said if it was that big I should be able to do it to myself.

INT. EDGAR'S TRAILER; NIGHT

Edgar enters the trailer with a newspaper in his hand. He tosses the paper onto the dinette table and gets a beer from the refrigerator. He notices the flashing light on his answering machine and taps the button.

ANSWERING MACHINE (through speaker)
You have four new messages. First new message. Tuesday, nine twenty-four PM.

PAM'S VOICE
Edgar, last shot at this before I go somewhere else. Please meet me at Wally's tonight.

ANSWERING MACHINE
Second new message. Tuesday, eleven forty-nine AM.

PAM'S VOICE (through speaker)
It's around noon, Edgar. I've been sitting in front of your trailer for an hour. You won't call back and you're not home. I don't know if you even...

He clicks the button for next message. It's a hang up and a dial tone. He clicks for next message.

ANSWERING MACHINE
Forth new message. Monday, four ten PM.

PAM'S VOICE
Been over a week since you said I wasn't a whore. Gonna sweet talk a
girl like that you should at least return her calls. Well...

Edgar clicks off the machine, sits at the table and unfolds the paper. He
scans a few lines then turns a page. He takes a swig of beer, then scans
and turns.

EDGAR (mutters)
Shit.

He gets up and leaves the trailer.

INT. WALLY'S TAVERN; SAME NIGHT

The bar is loud but not filled. Edgar enters and looks around. Pam isn't
there. He sees Too-Tall, the lumberjack, leaning against the bar with two
friends.

EDGAR
Remember me?

TOO-TALL
Nah.

EDGAR
I was here the other night with my brother and the cute red head. Too-
Tall cocks his head then sticks his finger into Edgar's chest.

TOO-TALL
Top. Yeah. You're the dude who stomped that big mouth at the
Division shindig?

EDGAR
Yeah. You see Pam, er Top, here tonight?

TOO-TALL
Nope. Hey, that was hot stuff out there, brother.

Edgar nods and looks around again. He takes an empty table in the back.
Sergeant Stone is sitting at the end of the bar. He watches Edgar as he sip
his beer. Slowly he rises and heads over to the table. Edgar looks up just
before he arrives. Stone stands above him, silently.

STONE
Let me buy you a round, Rittenauer.

EDGAR
No thanks.

Stone sits. The waitress comes over. Stone pulls a five dollar bill from
his jeans pocket and hands it to her.

STONE
Whatever the man wants. Keep the change.

EDGAR
I'm fine, thanks.

The waitress shrugs and hands the bill back to Stone.

STONE
That was pretty rude.

EDGAR
Yeah, well, I'm not staying.

STONE
Why come to a bar and not drink?

Edgar ignores him.

STONE
Waiting for someone?

EDGAR
Yeah, as a matter of fact I am.

STONE
Why don't we shoot the bull till she comes.

EDGAR
What makes you think it's a she?

STONE
Just a guess. Think you can take me down again?

EDGAR
What?

STONE
You heard me.

EDGAR
I'm outta your little club, okay, so why don't you buy yourself a life.

Stone nods and smiles. He stands and slowly walks around the table to where Edgar is still seated. He reaches down and grabs Edgar around his elbow, his thumb pressing into the ulnar nerve. Edgar winces but is determined not to show the pain. Stone squeezes harder.

STONE
We're not some little club, boy, and you're doin' yourself a healthy thing by runnin' out.

EDGAR
Better let go now.

(O.S) A voice behind Stone.

VOICE
Is there a problem?

Stone looks over his shoulder. It's Too-Tall.

STONE
What's it to you?

TOO-TALL
I am my brother's keeper.

Stone lets go.

STONE
Brother. Shit. Don't waste time waiting around here, Rittenauer.

EDGAR
What's that mean?

STONE
Doesn't really matter, does it. At least not now.

INT. MILITIA TRAINING AREA; ADLER'S AIRSTREAM; NIGHT

Adler, Byrd and Tony Rittenauer are sitting in Adler's office. All are in civilian attire.

ADLER (to Tony)
What do you know about the team?

TONY
Just that their training's a cut above.

ADLER
That important to you?

TONY
Sir, no disrespect to your unit but the only thing these soldiers can do is

shoot. If that's all I wanted to do, I'd have joined a gun club.

ADLER
Son, I've watched you, as has Captain Byrd. Tactically, we can use you, but politically I'm not sure.

TONY
Sir, I don't understand.

ADLER
Son, if I was to tell you that at this moment there were fifty-five men in a room hammering out a new, and never before implemented form of government, designed for us all, from the filthy rich to the filthy poor, how would you greet such news? With awe and amazement? With trust? Or with skepticism that fifty-five men could ever get it together enough to do battle for the betterment of us all?

Tony moves to speak.

ADLER
Let me guess how'd you answer. You'd be the former. You'd be a believer because you're still part of the uninitiated. But you'd have to question that such men could even exist, nevermind band together for such a noble effort. And you'd be right. So forget eighth-grade history and wonder if you will, if fifty-five men just two hundred years ago could seriously come together to create a government by the people and for the people.

TONY
As far as I know, that's how it all started.

ADLER
I'm glad you do, son. Because we can be about that. We are not destined to be about drilling in the woods on weekends, anymore than the Minutemen were destined to hide behind rock walls. And it's time we as a people begin to understand that we are on borrowed time. We have no morale compass. We have no fortitude. We have no sense of our own destiny. We are sheep being led by treacherous shepherds. There is a serious misconception about this country, son. First off, we

stole it from England, who stole it from Spain. Those who colonized it wanted it all. And who were the colonists? The street rabble? The laborers, hunters, farmers, fisherman? No. It was the landowners, the merchants, the captains of trade and industry, just as today. It was the new royal family without the coat of arms. Of course the rhetoric was marvelous, very meat and potatoes. It had to be. The Founding Fathers couldn't risk another revolution, against them this time. Well, it's two hundred and thirty years later, and I think we're ready to do it right.

Tony nods pensively.

TONY
We talking revolution here?

ADLER
No, son. This is about awakening the consciousness of America. We are a great people who have forgotten out heritage, not unlike the Native Americans whose cause the entire nation has taken up. Ironic, isn't it, that we are slowly neglecting our own.

TONY
I think I understand.

Adler leans across the desk.

ADLER
How much are you willing to learn, sergeant? How far are you willing to go?

17

INT. MCNAMARA FEDERAL BUILDING; FBI OFFICE, DETROIT; MORNING

Winston is at his desk. Osborne is in his office.

OSBORNE (yelling O.S.)
That cowboy here yet?

WINSTON
Haven't seen him.

Winston's phone rings.

WINSTON
Great. Be right there.

Winston pops in his head into Osborne's office.

WINSTON
Speak of the devil. He's out front.

OSBORNE
Is it just me or do you have a bad feeling about him?

WINSTON
He's wired different, but I suppose that's part of the game.

OSBORNE
He'd better rewire himself post haste, HQ endorsement or not. Get his funky ass in here.

Winston goes to the reception room office which has a large security window that's looks into the waiting room. He sees just one man, reading a copy of People magazine. The man is dressed in a tweed sportcoat and dockers; he's clean-shaven and his hair is neatly trimmed.

WINSTON (to Clerk)
That Chambers?

CLERK
That's the name he gave.

Winston walks around and opens the door to the waiting area.

WINSTON
Dexter?

He lowers the magazine.

CHAMBERS
Clean up pretty good, don't I?

INT. CRAIG OSBORNE'S OFFICE; DAY

DEXTER
Lotta angry folks in that line out there.

OSBORNE
You read the case summary yet?

DEXTER
Yep.

Dexter digs into his pocket and pulls out a cellophane wrap of Fig Newtons. He holds them out.

DEXTER
Fig Newton?

Winston waves him off.

OSBORNE
Questions?

DEXTER
Not really.

OSBORNE
Got it all, just from five lousy pages and some photos?

DEXTER
All I need for now. Sure you don't want one? Good breakfast food.

OSBORNE
You're acts getting a little stale with me, Chambers. Maybe you don't understand the gravity of this.

DEXTER
No, I understand the gravity of the situation. Remember, I'm the one that's gotta go in. Just that the important issues to you, like how I walk, talk, and look, aren't so damn important to me. See, I just got off an undercover with some nasty bikers. I was in a bar with them when they went nuts on a little Mexican girl. I snuck out and called for backup because I thought it was important stuff. But the men with the plan decided the whereabouts of a meth lab was more important than this poor little girl being gangbanged.

A secretary walks by the door. He holds out his coffee cup.

DEXTER
Hey, sweets, could you get me a refill on this. I'd do it myself but we're in this really important meeting.

She rolls her eyes and takes the cup.

DEXTER
Thanks, hun. You're a doll. Hey, give yourself a raise.

He turns back to Osborne.

DEXTER
Thing is, I'm good at what I do because of how I do it. If I wasn't, you know damn well I wouldn't be sitting here.

Chambers digs into the wrapper for another cookie.

WINSTON (TO CHAMBERS)
I may have another on the inside to help you – but it's speculative at this point.

DEXTER
If it ain't a young blonde, I'll go it alone, thanks.

WINSTON
Guy's name is Edgar Rittenauer… came in about a police chief up north. The DEA may be involved in that one.

DEXTER
Some unconfirmed snitch and another federal bureaucracy – all on the same page? No thanks.

WINSTON
The contact we've already set up, Jason Byrd… we can probably tag him with impersonating a DEA agent. That's a felony – ten large. So we've got him by the balls.

DEXTER
Now why the hell would he go do something like that? I know real DEA agents who won't admit what they do for a living.

WINSTON
To hide some coke, allegedly. But don't rely on him – it's not a given.

DEXTER
Thanks for the supporting cast, but I'm going to go solo. Them setting up phantom terrorist attack – not such a bad plan.

OSBORNE
Not a bad plan? Blowing up government buildings – not a bad plan?

Glad you weren't on McVeigh's jury.

DEXTER
It's a bad plan if you're on our side; not if you're on theirs. A group of lunatics seize upon a common enemy. Remember Waco, Ruby Ridge – when the militia groups were bad mouthing the feds? Janet Reno was a buffoon; everything was a conspiracy and everyone was involved? The fascist right and radical left can't do that now. The soldiers are darlings; the feds are doing the best they can to keep terrorists at bay. So suddenly, there's a new bad guy in town, someone even grandmothers in Sioux Falls would stand in line to choke. They're a perfect mark. And our government just keeps fueling the rage by letting them come in. Do you realize that since nine-eleven hundreds of thousands of visas have been issued to people from terrorist-supporting nations? Bet you the radicals know it. And Somalis, possibly some of the same thugs who slaughtered Task Force Ranger in Mogadishu have swarmed in Lewiston, Maine at an unhealthy rate, and are demanding housing and welfare that the town can't handle. And know what, the federal government is mandating that they be accommodated.

The secretary brings in his coffee. He smiles appreciatively.

DEXTER
Iraqi women are coming into this country to have babies and then go back home with our newest American citizen. The kids will be raised in terrorist training camps and allowed back into the U.S. when they reach killing age. All fact, no bull. Pissed? Yeah, people are pissed. Hell, I'm pissed. And you should be too. See, the administration went looking for weapons of mass destruction in Iraq to justify a war. Well, the militia's been looking for weapons too, and guess what? They found theirs.

OSBORNE
You sound like their poster child.

DEXTER
Not me. But most of middle America, like it or not, have the same gripes; high taxes, weak immigration laws, second amendment issues, moral disintegration, some of which I'm fine with.

WINSTON
But do you seriously think this militia's a national threat?

DEXTER
To over the government? Nah, no more then any terrorist group. But they can cause damage; and they can cause suspicion of all foreigners, which is what they want. They're coming off as the good guys, something they've never been seen as. People see them as protectors. They're a group of crazies with a cause, money and leadership – just like Al-Qaeda, or a biker gang. So yeah, they're scary.

INT. EDGAR'S TRAILER; DAY
Edgar calls Pam's work phone number.

EDGAR
Yes, please, I'm looking for Pam Trombley.

VOICE
She's not in yet.

EDGAR
It's past ten o'clock. She call in?

VOICE
No. Who's this?

Edgar hangs up and dials another number.

TONY'S VOICE
What are you doing calling me in the middle of the day? I work for a living, remember.

EDGAR
Yeah, great, have you seen…

TONY'S VOICE
Leave a message at the beep then go get yourself a job.

Edgar holds the phone away from his mouth.

EDGAR (mutters)
Dipstick.

EXT. PAM'S HOUSE; SAME DAY

Edgar parks his pick-up along the curb and walks casually up the driveway. He peers into the detached garage and sees her car. He begins casually up the back walk to her porch, then picks up the pace as he nears the door.

He knocks hard. No answer. He knocks hard again, then lowers his head to listen. Hearing nothing, he calls her name and rattles the doorknob which is locked. He calls her again. No answer. He rears back and kicks hard at the door – once, twice, until it gives way. He enters the kitchen yelling for her. He runs into the living room and stops short, his hands bracing himself at the narrow entryway. He looks down at her sprawled on the floor.

EDGAR (whispering)
Oh, Pam. I'm so sorry.

18

EXT. NEIGHBORHOOD ALLEY IN DETROIT; NIGHT

Tony Rittenauer is in civilian clothes, but he sports a BDU patrol cap, camouflaged face, and an AR-15 semiautomatic assault rifle. He is crouched behind a large dumpster, staring into the alley. The alley runs between the back of old, decrepit houses and detached garages, surrounded by mangled and rusted chain-link fences. Headlights turn into the alley and slowly approach.

He moves behind the dumpster. He is breathing hard and sweating, nervous as can be.

The car passes, rap music blaring from inside. As the taillights glow at the end of the alley and turn left, he hears someone approaching. He duck walks back out to the front of the dumpster and sees Sergeant Stone.

Stone is dressed in civilian attire, too, though a pistol adorns his left side.

STONE
Look a little more alive out here, Rittenauer. I could have slit your throat.

TONY
Yes, Sergeant.

STONE
This time it was just some neighborhood spooks passing through.

TONY
What do I do if I'm spotted?

STONE
What do you think that thing's for? Is it on safe?

TONY
Yeah. You serious, you want me to light them up?

Stone pulls the rifle away to check it

STONE
Fuck no, you'd screw up the entire mission, so keep alert and outta sight.

He hands the rifle back.

STONE
And keep your hand away from the trigger guard – you'll blow your damn hand off.

Tony clenches his jaw.

STONE
Got a problem?

TONY
No, Sergeant.

STONE
Wait for your signal.

Stone dashes back into the darkness. Tony watches him as he disappears. He peers out as drizzle turns to rain. He doffs his cap and shakes water from it. As he replaces it on his head, he sees a red flash blinking at the end of the alley. He pops up, looks left, the right, and quickly dashes towards the light.

STONE (O.S.)
Where the hell you going?

Stone is standing in the middle of the alley, ten yards behind Tony. Tony stops and turns to him.

STONE
Wrong way.

Tony and Stone run to the other end of the alley and get there just as a van slows and the back door opens. Stone jumps in first, then Tony. The door nearly closes on Tony's legs.

He crawls unsteadily to an empty spot near the passenger's compartment. As he turns, his rifle tangling momentarily under him, Stone, slightly out-of-breath, beads of perspiration on his camouflaged face, scowls at him.

EXT. MILITIA TRAINING AREA; NIGHT
The van sits parked in the dark, eight members from the special operations team around it. Captain Byrd is one. He is packing loose stacks of money and small packages of cocaine into small plastic containers. Tony is leaning against a tree, away from the van and the others. Stone is eyeing him. He approaches Tony.

STONE
You got a lot to learn, wonder boy.

Tony lowers his head and walks away.

STONE
Hey, I'm talking to you. You hear me, Rittenauer?

Tony turns to face Stone.

TONY
I'm tired of you Stone. You got a worthwhile critique, I'm all ears. If not, you can kiss my ass.

As Tony turns his back to Stone, Stone reaches up and grabs his shoulder, spinning him hard with one, clean jerk. Tony reflexively throws his arm up to block a punch, but Stone pulls him forward and drives his knee into his midsection. Tony doubles over. He puts a knee and his hands on the ground while he struggles to catch his breath. Stone stands over him. A small semi-circle forms around the two.

STONE
You up for that rematch, Rittenauer?

TONY (gasping)
What rematch?

Captain Byrd steps between them.

BYRD
What the hell's going on?

STONE
This clown took a swing at me.

Byrd looks around for witnesses. The others shrug. Tony struggles to his feet, unassisted.

TONY
Bullshit.

STONE
That's right. 'Cause I put you down before you got the chance.

A set of headlights illuminates the area. Byrd turns to see the vehicle, a black Chevy Tahoe. Frantically he addresses his men.

BYRD
Shit. Get that truck turned around ASAP.

Five soldiers scramble towards the truck. Byrd, Stone, and Tony watch as the driver exits when confronted. His hands on his hips, the driver looks around casually. He cannot be heard as he addresses the soldier. The soldier returns to Captain Byrd.

SOLDIER
Says his name's nobody's business but yours, sir.

BYRD
What's that?

SOLDIER
That's what he said, sir. And he called you by name.

Byrd stares at the man, then walks to him. Sergeant Stone follows close behind. He turns hastily, angrily to Stone.

BYRD
Wait here.

Byrd comes up from behind and talks to the man's backside.

BYRD
State your business.

MAN
Your mountain man sent me.

Byrd walks around to the man's front.

BYRD
Move back into the light.

The man moves into his headlights while Byrd watches him. It's Dexter Chambers.

BYRD
Carson?

CHAMBERS
No, me Cartwright, you Byrd.

BYRD
Get back in the truck, Cartwright.

Chambers does as directed. He watches as Byrd goes over to his men and gives some instructions before returning. Byrd jumps into the passenger's seat.

BYRD
Turn around and drive.

Chambers reverses the SUV and pulls out in the direction he came. Byrd turns on the radio. It's tuned to country-western.

CHAMBERS
Came along just to check out the stereo system? Hate to disappoint you but the truck's not for sale.

Byrd ignores him for a few seconds.

BYRD
You wired?

CHAMBERS
No, but I had a mighty strong Seven and Seven at dinner.

BYRD
Truck wired?

CHAMBERS
Yeah, it is a truck – headlights and all. What's your problem?

BYRD
I told my boy I didn't want you here till midnight.

CHAMBERS
So I'm eager. Some people might consider that a good thing.

BYRD
Yeah, well, I'm a cop, and I consider that a suspicious thing. How do you know mountain man?

CHAMBERS
First off, I know that's his screen name. Real name's Larry Simmons, your battle buddy from Tenth Mountain. But you asked how I know

him. Well, let's just say we've done a lot of business together.

BYRD
Describe him.

CHAMBERS
Early thirties, I'd say. Never did expect we'd be exchanging birthday cards. Short, 'bout five-nine. And thin – a sickly looking guy. Has long hair now, and a gold cross earring.

BYRD
Scars, marks, tattoos?

CHAMBERS
Bad job of a devil on his left shoulder.

Byrd smirks.

BYRD
Yeah. Got that on leave in Micronesia.

CHAMBERS
Never told me where.

BYRD
All right, so you and him have secrets. How come he hooked you up with us?

CHAMBERS
It's time to get back to work. I was in Angola and then Honduras.

BYRD
What unit?

CHAMBERS
No unit. I came in for my three years with the twenty-fourth Mech then went to work. You know?

BYRD
Yeah. I know. He tell you what we're about?

CHAMBERS
If he had, I wouldn't have trusted you enough to even show up.

Byrd stares out the side window for a few seconds, then turns to Chambers.

BYRD
How do you cross danger area?

CHAMBERS
Linear or area?

BYRD
What's an FPF?

CHAMBERS
Final protective fire.

BYRD
Set me up an ambush site.

CHAMBERS
I like the L-shape. Finished with AIT one-oh-one?

BYRD
For now.

CHAMBERS
Good, 'cause what I am is an ordinance man.

BYRD
Yeah? Simmons didn't tell me that.

CHAMBERS
'Cause I didn't tell him. It's not something you talk about to liven up the

party.

CHAMBERS

BYRD
We don't do bombs.

CHAMBERS
No one does, do they? I just need is a place to keep my skills sharp while I wait for work. I got the equipment, just need people who can stay out of the way and keep quiet.

BYRD
What's your specialty?

CHAMBERS
Work with them all; high and low. And fast velocity det cord, up to nine thousand meters per second. Slower shit too – when it fits the need.

BYRD
Yards.

CHAMBERS
What?

BYRD
It's yards here, not meters.

Chambers rolls his eyes.

CHAMBERS
Sure. I work with TNT and wax but mainly cyclonite; that's the plastic stuff. I used torpex once; scared the shit outta me. It's mainly for underwater blows and I can't swim a stroke.

BYRD
Ever work with nitrates?

CHAMBERS
Yeah. But it's bush. There's no control and it makes a mess.

BYRD
Sometimes, Mister Cartwright, that's what's needed.

INT. DEXTER CHAMBER'S UNDERCOVER HOUSE; KITCHEN;
NIGHT

Winston is at the table, drinking coffee. Dexter is sitting on the counter
eating a banana.

DEXTER
You liked that one, huh?

WINSTON
Yeah. What was it? Cyanide? Something like that?

DEXTER
Cyclonite.

WINSTON
What is it?

DEXTER
Dunno. Some kind of plastic explosive.

WINSTON
What about Torpex?

DEXTER
Not a clue, but I know they use it underwater. And I'm glad Byrd didn't
press me – I can't even light a Tiki lamp.

WINSTON
Area you telling me that all that crap about ambushes and det cord was
bullshit?

DEXTER
No, I don't lie; I just misrepresent. I went on-line at the airport when I
was coming up here and scoped out some Army field manuals. These

guys being into loud noises, I figured bombs who be a good backstop. I threw in the det cord for the arousal factor.

WINSTON
You have a photographic memory?

DEXTER
Nah, I just pay attention. Catch you off guard when he called me Carson?

WINSTON
No, I think you had him pretty tight by then. He just had to toss one more barb – see if he could trip you up.

DEXTER
What about when he asked where Simmons got his tattoo? Shit, how why would I know that – unless I was trying bullshit him.

WINSTON
No offense to that ironclad memory but better get all that written into a report, case the recorder had a meltdown on us.

DEXTER
Be in your boss's manicured little hands next time we meet. You said you've pegged this guy in a dope case?

WINSTON
Pretty sure.

DEXTER
Well, he's about a lot more than dope.

19

EXT. CEMETERY; PAM'S FUNERAL; DAY

Edgar is standing alone under a tree. About one hundred members of the Michigan militia are standing around the gravesite, heads bowed, listening to final prayers. Adler is there in dress blues, most others are in civilian clothes. Edgar watches as the crowd breaks up and Adler is escorted by his staff to a waiting Lincoln Towncar. The media intercepts him.

REPORTER
Colonel Adler, is it true that your unit has been approached by several neighborhood watch committees, as well as by several State Representatives, to assist in local homeland security.

Adler stops and addresses the media

ADLER
Ladies, gentlemen, this is certainly not a good time. We have lost a devoted and dedicated soldier.

SECOND REPORTER
But in light of this murder, do you feel your services are warranted?

ADLER
The police are certainly more suited to handle this matter.

REPORTER
But you have been approached; California and Florida militia units are saying that you'll soon follow them is conducting active patrols.

ADLER
Okay, folks, I guess it's no secret. We've been asked, and coordination is underway, but only on a limited scale. Unlike California and Florida, we've had no attacks here. And we're thankful for that. Now if you'll excuse me...

Adler is moved into his Towncar as Edgar watches from a distance.

EXT. EDGAR RITTENAUER'S PICK-UP TRUCK; DAY

Edgar is sitting in his truck on the crest of a ridge on a newly-paved boulevard. He is looking through the windshield into a shallow valley at a construction site. Edgar slowly drives down boulevard, past a sign that reads, "Welcome to Placid Valley, another fine Citadel Homes family community."

He pulls up to a group of Guatemalan bricklayers at work and leans out the window.

EDGAR
Any one know Tony Rittenauer?

They all look over though none stop working. An older worker steps nearer the truck.

WORKER
Sorry. Who?

EDGAR
Tony Rittenauer.

WORKER
What does he do?

Edgar scratches his chin.

EDGAR
I guess I don't know.

WORKER
Better you check over at the trailer.

Edgar nods. A short drive later, he sees Tony hauling two-by-fours off a truck. He puts his head out the rolled-down window.

EDGAR (yelling)
Tony.

Tony turns and nods but continues with his load until he can lean them against the skeleton of a house. He jogs over to the truck and leans into the open passenger's window.

EDGAR
Carpenter, huh?

TONY
No, not yet.

EDGAR
Eat lunch?

TONY
No, but I brown-bag it, eat with the guys. Hey, you call about that job?

EDGAR
No. Didn't see you at Pam's funeral

TONY
Work.

EDGAR
Sure. You still with those guys?

TONY
Who? The militia? Yeah, but not with Alpha Company; I... I'm sort of onto a new thing.

Edgar looks away, shakes his head, and gives an expression of contempt.

TONY
None of your business what I do, Edgar.

EDGAR
I know you're pissed, but you should of been there.

TONY
That's not what it was.

EDGAR
Get in.

Tony straightens up and looks away.

TONY
I told ya, I'm working.

Edgar sighs and slowly gets out and walks around to join Tony. He points up to the ridge he just descended.

EDGAR
Use to pheasant hunt this field, 'member, 'bout twenty, twenty-five years ago. You got your first one just over that ridge.

TONY
Remember the rifle – that beat up, old twenty-two dad left behind?

EDGAR
Yeah.

TONY
Those older kids made fun of it and took it from me, then smashed the stock on a rock. Splintered it to shit. I was so pissed. I was what, nine? And you were twelve, and had all the answers. You came out, saw me crying, and I knew you'd take care of those guys. Remember what you did?

EDGAR
I brought the gun home and taped it back together.

TONY
Told me it was as good as new and to let it go. You said they'd get tired of fucking with me and then it would be all right. You know, I thought you were scared.

EDGAR
They left you alone, right?

TONY
Physically, yeah. But they've never really gone away. You can't just tape up every problem and make it to go away... not Pam's death, not dad's running away, not....

Edgar walks a few feet away and looks around at the ridges surrounding him.

Tony, you're getting caught up in what's out there. Some of it's your concern, most of it's not. They're in the hills, and they've got you holding the low ground. That's not a safe place to be. You could do a whole lot more looking out for those closest to you.

TONY
Like dad?

Edgar turns to face him.

EDGAR
Yeah, like dad.

TONY
And what did that get you? Almost convicted.

EDGAR
Tony, I wouldn't have been convicted.

TONY
You sure?

EDGAR
Yeah. I was the DEA snitch who brought the cops inside.

TONY
What?

EDGAR
I found one guy doing a deal in the back and they started paying me off to keep my mouth shut. I thought they were just doing a little dealing in the streets. I took a spin in one of the rides, a souped-up Grand National. Flint cops stopped me carrying two keys in the trunk. Two keys. That's life without parole. So I spilled my guts.

TONY
You turned on our father?

EDGAR
No, he wasn't involved – and I told them that. He didn't know shit about it.

TONY
Then how'd the get him?

EDGAR
Everybody pled.

TONY
The feds never gave you up?

EDGAR
They didn't have to. Like I said, they all pled. The dopers gave statements that he let them run their business for a cut of the profits. After that, didn't matter what I said – being his son and all.

TONY
So why didn't you tell him to go to trial and testify for him?

Edgar puts his head down and kicks the dirt

EDGAR
I guess I hoped I could just tape it up and make it go away.

20

INT. MILITIA TRAINING AREA; ADLER'S AIRSTREAM; DAY

Captain Byrd and Colonel Adler are in the office in civilian clothes.

ADLER (annoyed)
I don't get it, Jason, it's not like you to be so loose with security.

BYRD
I didn't give him anything; I just didn't show him the door.

ADLER
I think you should do just that, and discreetly so that he doesn't get suspicious of our activities.

BYRD
Sir, I'd like to bring him in.

ADLER
No. You twisted my arm with Rittenauer, but we're five days from D-Day. I don't want fresh troops, especially untested ones.

BYRD
I can't get into his active duty file, but I have contacts who can check out his Angola and Honduras stories.

ADLER
In five days?

BYRD
No. But I don't need him for the first go 'round.

ADLER
Why do you need him at all?

BYRD
Sir, Stone has to go. The other night he laid into Rittenauer. I mean with knees and elbows. I can't have the rest of the team on edge.

ADLER
And are they? No one's come to me with any complaints.

BYRD
Because they're good soldiers, sir.

ADLER
I see no issue, Jason. Stone stays; you want, I can keep the other fella around in another unit until he's checked out.

The phone rings. Adler holds up his hand as he answers the phone.

ADLER
Citadel Homes.

P.O.V. changes to Sergeant Stone who is calling from a pay phone.

STONE
It's me.

ADLER
Hold it a sec.

Adler places his hand over the receiver.

ADLER
Anything else, Jason?

Byrd stands sharply.

BYRD
No, sir

ADLER
Then carry on, son.

Byrd nods once and departs.

ADLER (back to Stone, annoyed)
You got anything yet?

STONE
A hunch.

ADLER
Stone, I don't work on hunches. Where are you calling from anyway?

STONE
Relax, I'm on a payphone.

ADLER
Is your hunch a person or a place?

STONE
Person.

ADLER
I want a name.

STONE
Not yet.

Adler pounds the desk.

ADLER
A name, dammit.

STONE
Rittenauer.

ADLER
Shit. The new guy on the team?

STONE
No, his candy-ass brother. She called him on the phone that night.

Adler gets flush and rubs his chin. He sits up straight in the chair and breathes deep.

STONE
Colonel, you there?

ADLER
Yeah, yeah. Okay. Ah, follow him. But I want the OpOrder. Don't make a freakin' mess of it like like the last time.

STONE
If I make him gone, it don't matter about the order.

ADLER
Damn you, it does matter. We don't need another member going out for nothing.

STONE (angry)
Hey, that wasn't for nothing. You called me, remember. She gave it up to you, and then you gave it up to her – so don't go off making like I'm some homicidal maniac out for kicks.

Adler sets the phone down in his lap, closes his eyes, and tilts his head toward the ceiling.

STONE (O.C.)
You hear me. Hey, you still there?

EXT. MILITIA TRAINING AREA; RIFLE RANGE; DAY

The special operations team is on the line. Byrd walks over to Dexter Chambers who is observing and pulls him aside.

BYRD
I talked with my superiors and they feel it's best to put you in a line company for now.

CHAMBERS
What? Have you checked me out?

BYRD
Some. I called Simmons and you're solid. But, they like to observe the new talent before making a final decision.

CHAMBERS
Hey, I've come a long way to find a unit I can work with and it ain't them. I've met some of those line yokels over at Wally's the last few nights. You know they wanted me to settle a bet on whether the moon landing was staged. And you've got groups of guys out there examining highway signs for encrypted codes? Yeah – said they're directions for UN troops when the New World order rolls in. I'll tell you, Byrd, you got some kooks out there.

BYRD
You wanna stay, you'll be running with them for the time being. But I can use you, soon as things straighten out.

CHAMBERS
What things?

BYRD
Internal issues. You served, you know the drills. Hey, make you feel like part of the team, you can patrol the county as part of the militia initiative.

CHAMBERS (sarcastically)
Damn, Captain, I'm speechless.

Edgar's pick-up races into the lot and grinds to a stop, kicking up dirt and gravel. He jumps out and walks over to the group. The line stops firing and all direct their attention to him. Tony puts his hands on his hips and mouths "shit."

BYRD
Who the hell are you?

EDGAR
Me and him are gonna talk.

He points to Stone.

BYRD
You know this guy, sergeant?

STONE
Yeah, Rittenaur and I know each other.

Byrd looks over at Tony.

BYRD
You related?

TONY
Yes, sir. Brothers.

BYRD
Well, Rittenauer, this is private property. You have personal business with one of the men, it'll have to wait till he's done here.

EDGAR
I'd never call that bitch a man.

Stone struts forward, rifle at port arms. Suddenly and forcefully, Stone flips his rifle at Edgar who catches it.

STONE
Do it, cream puff, show us your stuff.

Edgar holds the rifle, barrel at a 45 degree angle, and stares at Stone for a few moments. Just as suddenly and forcefully, he throws it back at Stone.

EDGAR
I got nothing to prove to you, just something to prove about you.

Stones turns red and furious, and steps defiantly towards Edgar. He is held off by Byrd and Dexter.

STONE
You got a big mouth, know that Rittenauer.

Edgar smiles and nods perceptively.

EDGAR
Don't I though.

BYRD
This is private property. Leave. Now.

Edgar walks off the firing range.

STONE
Hey, Rittenauer.

Edgar turns. Stone has his rifle pointed at Edgar who stands before him brazenly. Quickly, Stone turns down range and fires an automatic burst that blows apart a squirrel sitting on a fallen tree branch thirty yards away. When Stone turns and flashes a sardonic smile, Edgar is standing by his truck, glaring, not at Stone, but at Tony, who glares back.

21

INT. WALLY'S BAR; NIGHT

Edgar is sitting alone at the bar, nursing a fifth of Jack Daniels. The bottle is half empty and Edgar is obviously feeling its effects. He is slumped and bleary-eyed. He turns to a man sitting next to him. This man is older. He's wearing a flannel shirt, cut off at the shoulders. His "CAT" hat is set low over his forehead. Edgar turns to him.

EDGAR
Hey, you with the militia?

The man looks over at him.

MAN
Nah.

EDGAR
Thought everybody in this place was with them.

MAN
You?

Edgar takes a drink.

EDGAR
Nah. Hey, what do you do?

MAN
Farmer.

EDGAR
Tough racket.

MAN
Yeah.

EDGAR
Should join the MILITIA (loudly). Everybody with a bitch joins the
MILITIA (loudly).

MAN
Relax, buddy.

Edgar fills his glass.

EDGAR
The MILITIA'S (loudly) a friend to everyone.

He turns around from the bar and slips off his stool, full glass in hand.
He addresses the bar. Some stop and listen, others turn their backs,
others continue to play pool.

Right, guys. Hey, I saw you all out there at the funeral. Oh yeah. All
quiet and church-like. Real brothers-in-arms.

Turns to the man beside him and slaps his back.

Hey, farmboy – you should of seen it. Real touching. Got me right here.

Bangs his heart with fist.

Now you're all in here getting drunk and ready to go out on the streets to
protect us all from... I don't know – bogeymen. Course, Pam
Trombley's murderer is out on there, too. Wait a minute, is he?

Edgar peers around the bar.

EDGAR
Yup, he's out there. Maybe you suckers can...

The man beside him grabs his arm.

MAN
C'mon buddy, that's enough.

Edgar pulls away and backs toward the door, waving his finger at the man.

EDGAR
No, no, no, you can't touch me.   I'm just drunk, but you're all fucking nuts.

Edgar stumbles out of the bar, into the parking lot, over to his car which he has a hard time finding. He pulls out of parking lot slowly and unsteadily with stops and starts. A ways down he's swerving over the center line. Realizing he's in no condition to drive, he pulls down a narrow dirt road with no traffic.

He doses off at the wheel and wakes up in time to see himself crashing into a tree.

EXT. EDGAR'S PICK-UP TRUCK; MORNING

Edgar is asleep, his forehead resting on the steering wheel. Drool is seeping from his mouth. Birds can be heard. He lifts his head and looks into the rearview mirror at himself.

He crawls out of the truck and staggers to the front of it. He's in a shallow ravine. The front end of his truck is creased against a thin tree.

He gets back in, starts it up, and is able to back out after flooring it and kicking up mud and tufts of grass.

He parks in front of his trailer and slowly climbs the short wooden steps to the door. He unlocks and opens it, throwing his keys on the kitchen table as he enters. He opens the refrigerator, takes out a beer, looks at it, then puts it back.

He walks into his bedroom and takes a black .38 caliber revolver out of the drawer and carries it back into the living area. He plops down on the dilapidated sofa and holds the revolver in his lap, twirling it by the trigger guard.

He unlocks the cylinder and checks for all six have rounds. He then stands up, with the revolver cylinder open, and clicks on his telephone answering machine.

As the machine comes on, he returns to the sofa, flipping the cylinder shut as he sits back down.

ANSWERING MACHINE
No new messages. Four saved messages. First saved message. Tuesday. Nine twenty-four PM.

PAM'S VOICE (through speaker)
Edgar, last shot at this before I go somewhere else. Please meet me at Wally's tonight.

He turns the gun towards his stomach with two hands and slowly raises it to his face.

ANSWERING MACHINE
Second saved message. Tuesday. Eleven forty-nine AM.

PAM'S VOICE
It's around noon, Edgar. I've been sitting in front of your trailer for an hour. You won't call me back and you're not home. I don't know if you even live here anymore. If you do, call. That Operation Trenton you were talking about, I was with… no, forget about how, but I got hold of it, and Edgar, if it's not just talk, this is big. I can't hold onto it much longer and I'm scared. They know I have it. I'm putting it in that safe place until I can get it to you, so please, please call.

Edgar stops and stares straight ahead as the answering machine plays on.

ANSWERING MACHINE
Third saved message. Monday. Nine-fifteen AM.

He jumps from the chair, leaving the revolver on the sofa.

As he races from the trailer, P.O.V. switches to a person sitting in a vehicle. As Edgar leaves the trailer park, CLOSE SHOT of the unknown person – Sergeant Avery Stone.

22

EXT. PAM'S HOUSE; BACK DOOR; DAY

The yellow evidence tape is still surrounding the house. Edgar is breathing heavily, though he moves painstakingly slow as he steps on the back porch. The door is locked. He picks up a fallen tree branch and looks around him. Quickly, he jabs the branch through the window and unlocks it. Sliding it up, he slips through and heads for the living room.

He stops in the doorway; the same spot he was when he found Pam. Dried blood stains the hardwood floors. He cuts through quickly and enters the back bedroom. He goes to the small closet which is loaded with stuff.

EDGAR (mumbling audibly)
Damn, girl, how did you expect to get a gun outta here in time?

He quickly pulls stuff from the closet, simultaneously feeling for loose boards. As he pulls out the shoe rack, the floor boards beneath move. Unable to peel them up with his fingers, he digs into them with one of his keys.

The slot is narrow and it's all he can do to dig his hand down into it. He pulls out the gun and tucks it into his waistband. Going back in, he wrestles out a thick, bound document rolled up and secured with rubber bands.

He breaks the bands and as it unravels he reads the title page: "OpTrent." He stands and flips through it randomly, mouthing the words as he reads.

EDGAR (muttering)
Holy shit.

EXT. DEXTER DRIVING DOWN A ROAD; DAY

Dexter is dressed in BDUs. He is on his cell phone.

DEXTER
Yeah, Winston, my boy, I'm dressed to kill. I get hard just looking at myself in the rearview mirror.

WINSTON
How are you hitting it off with Byrd?

DEXTER
I have a better chance with Britney Spears. But hey, I get to conduct roving patrols with...

Digs into his hip pocket and pulls out a slip of paper.

Sebastian Dudley. What do you think he goes by? Seb, Sebbie? Maybe I'll just call him Dud.

WINSTON
How long's you shift?

DEXTER
Shit, don't say it like that. Last time I did shift work was at Pizza Hut in Aberdeen, Washington.

They both snicker.

Hey, met your boy Edgar.

WINSTON
Where?

DEXTER
At the range – he declared war on the militia.

WINSTON
So he is tied to the militia. Maybe we can use him.

Dexter pulls into a parking lot already filled with soldiers and camera crews

DEXTER
Choke on that thought, boy. He's a bit too intense for me and not exactly their franchise player. Gotta go. I'll fill you in later; time to fight terrorism.

EXT. EDGAR'S TRAILER PARK; NIGHT

Edgar parks his truck, gets out and approaches his trailer. He sees a cardboard box on the trailer's steps. Reaching down, he picks up the box and stops in mid-bend before standing upright.

Holding the box extended, he sees a line connected to it. His arm shakes as he traces the line up to the door and over to a cylindrical cannister attached to the trailer at about head height.

Slowly he lowers the box. He is breathing heavily and sweating. He is watching the box and just as it is set on the concrete stoop, he hears the clang of metal on cement.

He looks over and sees the spoon of a hand grenade bounce. He turns just as the explosion comes.

EXT. SERGEANT STONE'S VEHICLE; NIGHT

He is watching across the street from the trailer park as neighbors swarm out to see what happened. Calmly, he picks up his cell phone and punches a button.

STONE
Done.

ADLER'S VOICE
Was this one another mess?

STONE
Not as bad as the one you created.

23

INT. TONY RITTENAUER'S HOUSE; NIGHT

Tony is sitting at the kitchen table. His web belt is on the table beside him as he packs a pair of binoculars into a fanny pack. There is an urgent knock on the front door. Tony moves casually to answer it as the knocking continues.

TONY
Yeah, yeah.

He opens the door just a fraction and it swings open violently into him. Edgar is on him, driving him to the floor. Edgar's shirt is torn, his face is blackened with dirt, and he's clearly pissed off. Tony attempts to wrestle him off.

EDGAR
I'm gonna pretend you don't know.

Tony stops struggling.

TONY (breathing heavily)
Know what?

EDGAR
What is Operation Trenton?

TONY
Never heard of it.

Edgar grabs the sides of his head and pounds him into the floor.

EDGAR
I know all the details except when.

TONY
I don't know what you…

Edgar pounds his head again, then slaps his face.

TONY
What the fuck can I say, I never heard . . .

Edgar moves off him, picks him up and pins him against a wall.

EDGAR
I've been thinking about it. Trenton. That was in New Jersey, where Washington crossed over the Delaware to surprise the Hessians on Christmas. Sneak attack right? Like this one. Only that didn't help me, I mean, what other type of attack would cowards like you conduct? So I did some research. It ended up the Cornwallis tried to sneak in on Washington a week later at Princeton, only George wasn't there. He had the tents set up and campfires burning but when the British came, no one was home. Washington had gone north to defeat Cornwallis' reinforcements.

TONY
What?

Tony tries to wiggle free but Edgar digs his forearm into Tony's neck.

EDGAR
They'll leave the campfires burning all night, you know, patrol the streets, save the cities. But they're actually sneaking out under the cover of darkness to do their dirty deeds.

TONY
Edgar get off me or so help me…

Edgar releases Tony, who sits down and rubs his neck.

EDGAR
They murdered Pam.

TONY
Who did?

EDGAR
Stone, probably.

TONY
Why? She was one of them.

EDGAR
No, she wasn't. Neither are you.

I found her, you know. Her head was damn near severed. That beautiful neck with that jagged slice, beautiful red hair sticky with blood.

TONY
Stop it.

EDGAR
She felt it. More painful than you or I could imagine. Paramedics said it took her at least five minutes to die. Those last minutes, knowing they were her last. She knew who and why. Just like we do. When's it going to happen, Tony?

Tony removes his BDU cap and stares at it in his hands.

TONY
Two in the morning.

EDGAR
Tomorrow?

TONY
I'm due at the staging area in two hours.

EDGAR
You can't go.

TONY

I have to. If I don't, they'll know something's up. And they'll kill dad, Edgar. They'll kill dad. They got guys on the inside who can make it happen. And they promised me they would.

24

INT. SMALL LOG CABIN; NIGHT

Byrd and Stone are in a back corner drinking coffee while several soldiers meander about. All are in civilian clothes.

BYRD (to Stone)
Rittenauer's out. But he's coming along to insure he stays quiet. That'll leave you a man short.

STONE
Why's that?

BYRD
He's too green. And that's all you need to know.

STONE
He was useless anyway.

Byrd hands him a slip of paper.

Dexter Cartwright will replace him. Call him at that number.

STONE
That new guy? I don't need him?

BYRD
The plan's laid out for ten bodies. It's weak on the outer perimeter as it is.

STONE
Fine. But I'll be on him like funk on a pig.

EXT. PAYPHONE; NIGHT
Edgar is calling.

VOICE
FBI Detroit.

EDGAR
I need to speak with Agent Ambrose.

VOICE
He's gone for the day, I'll give you his voice mail.

EDGAR
No, I need...

He hears an extension ringing and hangs up. He calls back.

VOICE
FBI Detroit.

EDGAR
I need to talk to Ambrose.

VOICE
Sir, I explained to...

EDGAR
No listen, this is an emergency. Get me to his house.

VOICE
Name please?

EDGAR
Edgar.

VOICE
Last name?

EDGAR
Just Edgar, he'll know.

Edgar waits impatiently as the call goes through.

EDGAR
C'mom, c'mon.

WINSTON'S VOICE
Edgar?

EDGAR
You said you'd pay for info on this group, that still the offer?

WINSTON'S VOICE
Yeah.

EDGAR
I don't want money. What I want is more important to me and should be easier for you to get. And don't ask me if this is for real – we ain't got time for games.

INT. DEXTER CHAMBER'S UNDERCOVER HOUSE; LIVING ROOM; NIGHT

Dexter is lying on the couch with beer and pretzels, watching a Hogan's Heroes rerun on television. There's an insistent knock at the door that startles him. He dumps the pretzels on the floor. He rolls off the couch and peers out the front window. He can't make it out but there's a big shadow on the door stoop. He takes his pistol from his ankle holster and puts it in his front pocket. He opens the door a crack, then wider when he sees who it is.

DEXTER
What's up?

STONE
Get your boots and a shirt on.

DEXTER
For what?

STONE
Captain Byrd requests your presence for the evening.

DEXTER
Why didn't he call me?

STONE
Unlike me, he likes surprises.

DEXTER
I'll get my things.

Dexter tries to close the door on Stone but Stone kicks his foot in.

STONE
I'll watch.

DEXTER
Suit yourself, but don't expect any action on the first date.

Stone stands expressionless in the door. Dexter grabs his boots off the floor and his BDU shirt from the railing. He sniffs it and shakes his head.

STONE
Civilian attire.

DEXTER
I thought this was a militia outing?

Stone remains silent.

DEXTER
Right, a surprise.

Dexter goes to his back bedroom. He turns to make sure Stone isn't
following. He takes the pistol from his pocket and deftly slides it into
the ankle holster. He tucks his FBI credentials into the sock of his other
leg. Quickly he puts on his boots while grabbing the portable telephone
and starts to make a call.

STONE
Who you calling?

DEXTER
A girlfriend. I was supposed to meet her tonight.

STONE
This late?

DEXTER
She's a dancer.

Stone stares at him.

STONE
Then I'm sure she'll find someone else. Move.

They walk out the door and into Stone's truck. Dexter's cell phone
rings.

DEXTER
See, she does love me.

He answers the phone.

DEXTER
Hey, love, missing me?

WINSTON
Thank God I caught you. I just a got a call. Something's up tonight and
. . .

DEXTER
Yeah, babe, I'm on my way out right now.

WINSTON
Out? Where?

DEXTER
Someplace special, I'm sure you know where.

Stone's snatches the phone from Dester, stares at the LCD readout for
caller id, and then tosses the phone out the driver's side window.

EXT. WOODED AREA; NIGHT

Men of the special operations team, dressed in civilian clothes, are
loading into the white cargo van. Tony Rittenauer attempts to enter the
rear but is blocked by Stone who glares down at him. Captain Byrd
walks over and tugs at Tony's shoulder. Tony backs off and the next
soldier enters the van.

TONY
What's the problem, captain.

BYRD
You're not on board with this one.

TONY
Why not?

BYRD
You'll be staying back with Major Grosmeyer. You're not to make a
phone call or leave this cabin until I get back. Understand?

TONY
You think I've gone over?

Stone moves between them.

STONE
You heard the captain. Get inside.

Tony moves off under the gaze of Stone as Dexter walks up to Byrd.

DEXTER
What's going on?

BYRD
You'll be with Sergeant Stone. Just pay attention and do as he says.
You do that, they'll be more.

DEXTER
More what?

STONE (to Byrd and Dexter)
Mount up, gentlemen.

Dexter climbs into the back of the van and Byrd enters the passenger's
side. The driver closes the rear door and the back is thrown into total
darkness. The driver enters the front seat, his door slams, he starts the
vehicle.

The van drives off. After a time, Dexter tries to stretch his legs out but
he meets resistance on the floor in front of him. Stone flashes a penlight
on a large vinyl bag. He reaches down and partially unzips it. He
flashes his light on the face of a dead Arab male with a scraggly beard
and mustache.

STONE (to Dexter)
Just in case the feds piece the bomber back together. Whataya think?

Stone turns the pen light on Dexter.

DEXTER
You know when they do those stories on serial killers, and they show photos of them as young kids, all smily and happy, you don't have one of them at your house, do you?

Stone flicks the light off.

DEXTER
Didn't think so.

They drive in dark and silence for a while.
The van cruises to a stop. Byrd turns around to the men in the back.

BYRD
Phase line green. Wait one. Hold up...

Sound of a car passing.

BYRD
Okay, go.

The back door opens and Stone jumps out. He points to two soldiers. The two climb out quickly and disappear into a dark parking lot. Dexter crawls out slowly. Stone closes the van door and the van speeds off with Byrd and the rest of the team. Dexter looks around. They are on the side of a road under a highway overpass. To their right is a dark covered parking lot. RUMBLINGS of an occasional vehicle is heard.

DEXTER
Where the hell are we?

Stone gives him a push.

STONE
Get going.

Dexter begins to walk forward, looking over his shoulder. When he sees Stone sprint by him, he jogs to keep up. The road disappears as they move away into the darkness. They reach a set of steps and go down.

Dexter can no longer see Stone, but he can hear the echo of footsteps in front of him. As Dexter ascends a second set of steps, Stone steps in front of him. He is barely out of breath; Dexter is startled. He takes the opportunity to bend over and try to catch his breath.

DEXTER
You... gonna tell me... where we're headed?

He looks up. Stone is gone. Dexter shakes his head and backs down the steps.

STONE
Where you think you're goin'?

DEXTER
I have no idea, but not much further if you don't fill me in.

STONE
We're outer perimeter.

DEXTER
Of what?

Stone points up.

STONE
Of that.

Dexter glances at the "GM" sign atop the Detroit Renaissance Center, then looks back at Stone. Stone nods his head, bidding him to move.

They reach Hart Plaza and the large central fountain. They cross quickly to the raised statue of Antoine de la Mothe Cadillac. Stone kneels beside it. Dexter does likewise. It begins to drizzle.

STONE
Stay here; man the radio.

Stone hands him a small, handheld radio.

STONE
We're all on the same freak. Your area of responsibility in everything from the river on your left to the steps we just came up. Your call sign is Alpha four. I'm Alpha one, and the only one you'll need to be talking to on this thing. Got it?

DEXTER
So far.

STONE
See anything, hear anything, let me know.

DEXTER
What's happening at GM headquarters?

STONE
Big party and we're the decorating crew.

Stone gets up to leave but Dexter holds him.

DEXTER
What?

STONE
We're blowing it, you dumbshit. We're blowing it and leaving our corpse behind to take the credit.

DEXTER
For what?

STONE
It's what we do. And now you're part of the biggest conspiracy ever on U.S. soil, so don't even think about going over.

Stone rushes behind towards the Ford Auditorium. Dexter waits and listens, then slowly moves from his position and circles around Hart

Plaza, being careful to stay in the shadows along the perimeter walls.

He squats and listens for a moment, then makes a dash for the steps. He is struck on the back of his head from behind and goes down. A knee goes into his back and the barrel of a pistol to his head. He is woozy and can't fight as hands squeeze him and search around his waist, and down his right leg to his boots. The hand pulls out the small semi-automatic from Dexter's ankle holster. Stone holds it in front of his face.

STONE
Glock. Shoulda known you'd carry a Kraut gun. What else we got?

Stone feels down the left leg to the boot.

STONE
A wallet? No, too big.

He pulls out Dexter's FBI credentials.

STONE
Won't this just be a kick in the balls to Byrd – his golden boy, a fed.

DEXTER (moaning)
Oh, shit.

STONE
That 'bout sums up your predicament, don't it? Call me all kinds of fool but don't ever underestimate my tactical competence.

Stone kneels down and presses his hand onto the side of Dexter's face, pressing it in the cement pavement.

Leans down to Dexter's ear.

STONE (sinister whisper)
Did you really believe I'd lay this whole plan out and then let you slip out the back door?

DEXTER (muffled)
Kind of hoping for that.

Stone looks up at the fountain.

STONE
This just might work out for everyone. What if I drill you in the back of
the head and take your Glock and badge back to Byrd, sorta like a scalp
as proof of what you were? Then, when you're found here and our dead
raghead is put back together, the boys in Washington think you got
whacked by a terrorist. And you get a hero's funeral. Like it?

Stone stands and moves in front of Dexter. Dexter lifts his face from the
pavement and looks up at Stone. Stone points the Glock at Dexter. A
GUNSHOT is heard. Dexter's eyes shoot open and he rolls over quickly.
He sees Stone laying in a pool of blood and brain matter.

VOICES
FBI! Down, down, down.

A helicopter swoops in and black clad FBI SWAT agents swarm him and
draw down with AR-15's. He sits with his knees drawn up to his chin
and lowers his head.

Across Hart Plaza, a man wearing a BDU patrol cap lowers his rifle and
stares out at the scene. It is Edgar Rittenauer.

EXT. JUST INSIDE THE RENAISSANCE LOBBY; NIGHT

Byrd is on a cell phone.

BYRD
Eagle down! Eagle down!

Two black-gloved hands grab his arms and pull him to the ground.
Winston Ambrose grabs the cell phone. He speaks into it.

WINSTON
Who is this?

Adler is sitting in his study. A dim banker's lamp illuminates his face.
He is speaking very calmly.

ADLER
Colonel Peter Adler, commander of the Sixth Brigade, Michigan militia.

WINSTON
Mister Adler, this is Special Agent Winston Ambrose of the FBI.

ADLER
Good morning, Agent Ambrose.

WINSTON
We have your men.

ADLER
I know. And if you don't have all you need by now, you soon will. You
people are amazingly adept at getting the facts too late.

WINSTON
Not this time.

ADLER
I'm afraid you're still too late, agent. All you've done is stop a small
group of patriots.

WINSTON
You're terrorists, Mister Adler, not patriots.

ADLER
Terrorists today, patriots tomorrow. We're both consumed with the same
goal; trying to prove to America how real the threat is. Except we nearly
did it.

WINSTON
What you've done is murder innocent people.

ADLER
Don't you understand – your way can't work? They were necessary victims – collateral damage. This country, with its weak spine, is just another terrorist-supporting nation. Look around, Ambrose, the enemy is growing bigger and stronger and smarter, and its within our borders. What it didn't accomplish in '93 it did in 2001. And it'll do it again.

WINSTON
That's because we have the best bicycle on the block. Most people admire it. Others throw rocks at it or try to steal it. But we ride it hard and fast and proud. It's our freedom, and freedom has it's enemies, Mister Adler. We fight damn had to live it and damn hard to protect it, and I won't apologize to anyone for that.

ADLER
Just understand, Agent Ambrose, that I am a patriot. And I'll leave with this thought. Ours was a fairly small operation; easy to unmask; our aim was to make America take notice, not create mass destruction. But they're different. You'd better be more committed to destroying them than they are to destroying you.

WINSTON
We are. Don't make the mistake of doubting that. Where are you?

ADLER
I'm at home.

WINSTON
Don't do anything foolish; we'll be down to get you.

Adler disconnects. He takes a sip of flavored water and slowly rises from his chair. He jots a short note down on a piece of paper and leaves it on the desk. He walks slowly through the house, shutting off each light. He walks into the garage and the door closes behind him. A few seconds later a GUNSHOT is heard.

INT. MCNAMARA FEDERAL BUILDING; DETROIT; DAY

Winston and Dexter are walking to the elevator.

WINSTON
Want me to thank Rittenauer for you?

DEXTER
No, I still think he was aiming for me.

Dexter steps into the elevator, leaving his back to Winston as the door closes. Winston smiles and shakes his head.

OVERHEAD PAGE
Special Agent Ambrose, you have a call on line three.

Winston hurries to the nearest phone and picks it up.

WINSTON
Ambrose.

CLOSE UP of the man on the other end, showing only his mouth and the brim of his BDU cap.

VOICE
Got that matter taken care of for me?

WINSTON
Yeah, we meet with the parole board in the morning. I think they'll go along with an early out for your dad. May be on a tether for a while, though.

EDGAR
How's Tony doing?

WINSTON
Stubborn, like you.

EDGAR
Then he'll come around.

WINSTON
It's his only way out.

EDGAR
Ever kill anyone, Ambrose?

WINSTON
No.

EDGAR
Could you?

WINSTON
I think so. Don't beat yourself up, it was a good shoot.

EDGAR
Yeah, well… You're not dealing with ordinary folks here. They won't talk… no matter what.

WINSTON
Sure they will. Just got to find the right motivation. That's all it takes.

EDGAR
Maybe so. But they won't know the whole story. Lucky for you, Casey Kittle of 812 Edgemont in Madison Heights does – and he's expecting you. He's got what you need to put it all together.

WINSTON
What's he know?

EDGAR
Not a damn thing. He's just an old man who didn't last a weekend out there. But later today he'll receive a sealed packet by personal courier.

He won't know what it is, and he'll try to open it. Be there when he does.

WINSTON
How'd you get hold of it?

EDGAR
Takes more than one person to save a nation.

WINSTON
Nah – that's all it takes. You're proof of that.

EDGAR
I'm just an American, that's all.

WINSTON
Yeah, well, I'll need for trial, Mr. America – so don't wander off.

EDGAR
The earth is round, Ambrose. No matter where I go, I'm no more than half a world away.

Both men smile as they hang up the phone.

EXT. FERRY TERMINAL; MICHIGAN; DAY

Edgar walks toward a small passenger ferry bound for Beaver Island, Michigan. Just before he boards, he takes off his BDU cap, examines it for a few seconds, and tosses it into a trashcan.

The ferry disembarking, a young boy walks by the trashcan, spots the cap, and retrieves it with a smile.